Scoring WITH THE WRONG TWIN

A WAGS NOVEL

D1522172

Scoring WITH THE WRONG TWIN

A WAGS NOVEL

NAIMA SIMONE

Copyright © 2018 by Naima Simone. All rights reserved, including the right to reproduce, distribute, or transmit in any form or by any means. For information regarding subsidiary rights, please contact the Publisher.

Entangled Publishing, LLC
2614 South Timberline Road
Suite 105, PMB 159
Fort Collins, CO 80525
Visit our website at www.entangledpublishing.com.

Brazen is an imprint of Entangled Publishing, LLC. For more information on our titles, visit www.brazenbooks.com.

Edited by Tracy Montoya
Cover design by Cover Couture
Cover art from iStock and Deposit Photos

Manufactured in the United States of America

First Edition January 2018

To Gary. 143.

Chapter One

"No." Sophia Cruz lifted her coffee mug to her lips, took a sip of air, and frowned down into the empty cup. When had she drunk the last of Puerto Rico's Greatest Gift to Mankind—otherwise known as Alto Grande Super Premium coffee?

Shoving back from her desk, she ignored her twin sister, who was perched on the end of the furniture giving Sophia her best puppy dog eyes, complete with slightly quivering bottom lip. "And you know that"—she drew a circle in the air in front of Giovanna's face as she passed by her toward the one-cup coffee maker—"isn't going to work on me. I taught you that trick."

Giovanna sighed, losing the woe-is-me expression. "Fine," she huffed, flipping her long, dark brown hair over a bare shoulder. "But, Fi, I seriously need your help. Pretty please?"

"Umm, hell to the no," Sophia reiterated. A press of the button, and the brew started streaming out of the machine with a hiss. The strong, heady aroma of ground coffee beans drifted upward, and she shamelessly—and noisily—inhaled.

Damn, that smelled good.

"Fi, this is more important than your next caffeine hit. God, can you at least pay attention?" Exasperation dripped from Giovanna's voice, but Sophia didn't turn to face her sister until the last drop hit the cup. Molding her fingers around the ceramic, she turned, and arching an eyebrow, peered at her identical twin over the rim.

Identical. Hah.

They might share the same Puerto Rican heritage, eye and hair color, facial structure, height, and body type, but that's where the similarities between them came to a screeching, skid-marked halt. Giovanna was all elegance and sophistication, with her expertly applied makeup, perfectly styled hair that framed her face and flowed over her shoulders, and an emerald romper that seemed to glow against her honey-toned skin and display her long, slim legs. As opposed to Sophia's cosmetic-free appearance, blue-tipped dark hair snatched up in a haphazard top knot, and the white wifebeater and ripped jeans she *might* have also worn yesterday.

Giovanna wore rings on her fingers and toes, and Sophia wore them in her eyebrow, bottom lip, and, uh, other body parts.

Her twin preferred art on her apartment walls; Sophia loved it inked into her skin.

Nope. It wasn't hard to guess which twin was the model and which sat at a computer developing apps at FamFit for a living.

And yet, for all their dissimilarities, Sophia loved Giovanna, and there was no one closer to her in the world. For twenty-four years—literally, since the womb—Giovanna had been her best friend. Didn't mean her younger sister by three minutes didn't ride her damn nerves like Lance Armstrong on a Trek mountain bike.

"Fi, this is for the House of Bianchi. *The House of Bianchi.* One of the hottest designers on the planet. And they want me to walk in their show. I can't turn this down. It's the most important job of my career so far."

Sophia shrugged. "So go."

Giovanna released a loud, long sigh that translated to *God, please give me the patience not to strangle this bitch.* Twin speak. A wonderful thing. "As I've been trying to explain, I already have a previously scheduled shoot with *Sports Unlimited* a day after I'm supposed to fly out to Milan. I can't be in two places at once."

"Not unless you want to dissolve into a gelatinous glob of goo before bursting into tiny particles." Sophia sipped her coffee, then frowned. "No, wait. That's only if you occupy the same space *and* time. My bad."

"I'm not going to comment on your obvious lack of understanding of the space-time continuum this one time because I need you. But fair warning, if I didn't, I would definitely advise you on the nil-to-none odds of you ever getting laid if you insist on spouting the flawed issues of the paradox in time travel."

Sophia gasped. "You bitch. You've been watching *Back to the Future* and *Time Cop* without me!" she accused.

The two of them might not agree on piercings, tattoos, or who was the hottest member of the Avengers—Iron Man, of course, although Thor ran a close second—but they shared the same obsession with eighties movies.

Giovanna rolled her eyes. "There was a marathon on TV the other night. I wasn't going to miss Marty McFly trying to avoid sexing his mother for you."

"Eew." Sophia screwed up her face.

Her twin sighed. "Focus for a minute. Please? Back to me."

"Nope." Sophia shook her head. "I don't want to focus,

because my answer is still no. Uh-uh. Forget it, *chica*. Not gonna happen. And, for when you get to Milan, I believe 'no' is the same in Italian."

"Fi…" her sister whined, but Sophia cut her off with another, firmer shake.

"No way. What you're suggesting is ridiculous. Just cancel the other shoot if the one in Italy is so damn important."

"I can't," Giovanna said, pushing herself off the desk. She paced the width of Sophia's small home office. Even frustrated, she still maintained the sultry prowl that had captured the notice and representation of her New York agency. Sophia couldn't imitate that strut, not even if Steve Jobs' ghost pulled a Jacob Marley and returned from the dead to offer her the corner office at Apple. "I committed to the *Sports Unlimited* shoot a year ago. It's their annual sexiest athletes edition, and not only is it too short notice to notify them, but it would be unprofessional to bail at the last minute. It only takes one mistake to be blackballed in this field, Fi. I've worked so hard to get where I'm actually requested by clients and photographers, but I'm not Gisele Bundchen. I can't afford to screw up either of these opportunities. Which means I have to make both of them."

"Damn it, Vanna," Sophia growled, setting the mug down behind her. She swept her hand over her hair, fingers bumping the topknot.

No one more than she knew how much Giovanna had worked in her chosen career. Some people might think being a model was frivolous or shallow, but since Giovanna was thirteen, she'd set her heart on being the next Adriana Lima or Arlenis Sosa. And Giovanna had directed her single-minded and sometimes intimidating focus toward her goal. In the last two years, she'd started to gain fame in the United States, booking more jobs, appearing on more covers, walking in more runway shows. Sophia admired her sister's grind and determination, celebrated her success. And she would do anything to support her, but this...

"I can't just take a day off work. You know Brian is on me twenty-four seven. He's just looking for another reason to write me up." Another reason besides her objecting to him claiming credit for her work, refusing to kiss his ass, and being a woman. Her supervisor was a real charmer. But if she ever wanted to open her own app development company one day, she had to deal with the bullshit at FamFit. At least until she earned enough money—and nerve—to strike out on her own.

"The shoot is in a week. If you ask for a vacation day now, even he can't say no," Giovanna countered.

Sophia groaned. "What you're asking is impossible."

Like a predator sensing the weakening struggle in its prey, Giovanna drew to a halt mid-pace and rushed over to Sophia. "No, it's not. We're identical twins, for chrissakes. No one would be able to tell the difference."

"Are you serious?" Sophia scoffed. "You're"—she waved a hand down her sister's elegant figure—"you. And I'm...me." She didn't go into further detail, because hell, there wasn't any need. Some things were just self-explanatory. Still, she tried. "Anyone would take a look at you—perfect hair, perfect figure—and immediately tell I'm not you. Supermodel Joan Smalls." She pointed at her twin then jabbed a thumb toward herself. "Igor."

"Oh please." Giovanna flicked a hand as if swatting away her words. "Put on some makeup, remove that hardware from your face, and add hairstyling..." Her eyes narrowed on the thick mass on top of Sophia's head.

"Hell no," she objected, grabbing the loose bun as if she could protect the strands from her sister. "I'm not getting rid of the blue. Not even for you. I might even love it more than you."

Giovanna smiled, and Sophia smacked her palm to her forehead. If she was already talking in terms of what she wouldn't do, then she was already halfway to relenting. And from the satisfaction in Giovanna's grin that could only be described as cat-who-ate-the-whole-damn-aviary, not just the canary, her twin had caught the slip.

"Oh, I'm sure we could make it work," she purred.

"Oh shit," Sophia muttered, closing her eyes. She'd just capitulated without even a valiant fight. "Just...shit. Okay, fine," she surrendered on a low groan. "I'll take your place on the sports shoot."

"Fi, thank you, thank you," Giovanna squealed. "And it won't be that bad, I promise. It's not until next week, so I'll give you a crash course on what you need to know. Hell, you might find you enjoy it." Giovanna hugged her tight, squeezing the breath from her. "Thank you," she whispered. "So much. I owe you one."

"Oh shut up," Sophia grumbled, returning the embrace.

Good God in heaven.

What the hell had she just agreed to?

Chapter Two

One week later, sitting in a director's chair while a woman with hair the color of a sunset caked what felt like a shitload of foundation on her face, Sophia repeated the same question to herself.

What the hell have I agreed to?

It was four o'clock in the afternoon. She should still be in her office at FamFit, working on their latest fitness app they hoped would give Fitbit a run for its money. Instead, she'd been in this Belltown photography studio since two in the afternoon, submitting to the handling of makeup artists, nail technicians, and hair and clothes stylists. Maybe most women would call this pampering, but not her. Torture. Enduring the slow dripping of water on top of her head might be worse than this…but not by much.

Christ. How had she let her sister convince her to do this? It's a simple shoot for *Sports Unlimited*'s annual sexiest athletes edition, Giovanna said. You'll be great, Giovanna said. This was crazy. Beyond crazy. Complete lunacy worthy of a stay in Arkham Asylum.

"I don't know what made you decide to color your tips blue, but I love it," Delia, the hairstylist, praised as she wound another lock of hair around the wide barrel of ceramic curlers. "They will look fabulous against the jersey."

"And the tattoo," Mona added, glossing Sophia's cheekbones with a big brush. "What happened, sweetie? Man trouble?" She shook her head, the huge auburn and gold afro quivering around her pretty face. "I almost covered it up, but then I thought it will look gorgeous with the outfit."

Sophia heard the rest of their conversation as if through a thick layer of cotton. *Holy shit.* Since the peacock tattoo wrapped low around her left hip bone, what the hell kind of outfit did Sheila have planned? When she'd gotten the ink two years ago, it'd been for her, not a man. The peacock had seemed the obvious choice. Vision, guidance…protection.

The purpose hadn't been to flaunt it in front of God and country.

Ohhhh Jesus, this was a mistake.

"Just a few more touches…" Mona murmured. A very short time later, she stepped back, surveying her handiwork. A wide smile stretched her vibrantly painted mouth. "Beautiful."

"I'm just about done, too," Delia announced, carefully setting the curlers on the stand next to them. She ran her fingers through Sophia's hair, twisting here, tucking there, before finally cupping her shoulders and turning her toward the lighted mirror.

Sophia sucked in a breath.

The woman who stared wide-eyed back at her was… stunning.

Big, loose waves tumbled around her face, emphasizing brown eyes that had always seemed average. Now, rimmed in black eyeliner and gold eyeshadow, they appeared darker, mysterious. She suddenly had cheekbones that would've made Kerry Washington grind her teeth in jealousy. And a dark red tint added a lushness to her mouth that almost embarrassed her. This was the mouth of a woman who owned her sensuality, reveled in it.

And liked to be kissed…a lot.

"Speechless." Delia snickered. "We must be damn good at our jobs."

Yeah, they deserved medals of valor. Because for the first time in her twenty-four years of being Giovanna Cruz's twin, Sophia actually felt as beautiful as her flawless sister.

"Here we go." Sheila, the clothes stylist, materialized behind them, holding up a child-size blue, white, and black jersey with the number 88 emblazoned on the front and… and…

She stared at the tiny piece of black cloth that could have generously been called shorts. Very generously.

I'm going to kill you, Giovanna.

"C'mon, hon," Sheila urged, gripping her elbow and propelling her out of the chair. "We don't have a lot of time."

Standing on rubbery legs, she moved behind a partition and wriggled into the shiny booty shorts, muttering under her breath.

And swallowed a groan.

The black, clingy material rode low on her hips, and the colorful bird rose above the band like a vibrant painting. But the hem of the shorts barely cleared the bottom of her ass. If she bent over, everyone would be a season ticketholder to her See You Next Tuesday.

Oh sweet baby Jesus.

Shaking her head, she reached for the jersey. Held up the cropped top.

"Umm." She peeked around the edge of the partition, careful to keep her bared torso hidden. "Is something supposed to go underneath this jersey?" Like a turtleneck.

"Of course," Sheila said, tsking. "I totally forgot." The stylist snatched a hanger off the rack and handed it to Sophia. "Here you go."

Dumbfounded, she stared at the black bra-style garment. The *Oh, hell no* quivered on her tongue like a notched arrow ready to fly. *Giovanna wouldn't have a problem wearing this. And for today, you're Giovanna. And sex sells.* The reminder didn't erase the first razor-tipped nails of panic from clawing at her throat.

In that moment, she was transported back years ago to a high-school girls' locker room where, naked and humiliated, she'd gathered her soaked clothes from the shower floor as a group of girls taunted her about her fat ass and dimpled thighs. The shame and helplessness swamped her. And for a long second, she froze, powerless against the ferocity of that memory, once more the heavier, uglier Cruz twin. That time in the shower, surrounded by jeering, snickering mean girls, had also been the last time she'd been naked in front of anyone. Even during sex, she wore a T-shirt or insisted on the dark.

And for all the skin the midriff-baring jersey and brief shorts revealed, she might as well be naked.

God. Briefly closing her eyes, she shuddered. She hadn't been prepared for this emotional backlash when she agreed to her sister's charade.

Man up, girlfriend. You're not that awkward teen anymore. They didn't break you then, and this skimpy outfit won't today.

Minutes later, jersey on, she inhaled a deep breath, pressed her palms to her belly, and straightened her shoulders. Ordinarily she wasn't a praying girl—Easter and Christmas Eve mass was more her speed—but today, she sent up a quick Our Father and followed up with a Hail Mary just to cover all bases.

Showtime.

The cool air of the studio brushed over her skin, raising goose bumps over her arms and legs. The squirming in her stomach hadn't ceased, but she smoothed her face into an impenetrable mask—another inheritance from high school—and followed Sheila down a short flight of stairs and into the main part of the studio.

Huge floor-to-ceiling windows took up one wall, and the afternoon light bathed the wide, open space. Her bare feet slid across the cool, smooth hardwood floors, and she ordered herself not to wrap her arms around herself. WWGD? *What Would Giovanna Do?* That was her mantra for the day.

Cameras, tripods, chairs, laptops, people—how many did it require to take pictures?—and huge white umbrella-looking stands littered the area. Carefully, she picked her way through the maze of cables, extension cords, and power strips as if they were a nest of reptiles ready to strike at her ankles.

Sheila paused at the edge of the organized chaos, and Sophia followed suit, mentally flipping through the poses her twin had taught her in a modeling crash course. *Hips tucked. Back arched. Smize.* She absently glanced at the huge backdrop dominating the wall...

Ay que papi mas lindo.

That man. *What a beautiful hottie.*

He was huge. Like Titans-roaming-the-earth-making-mountains-tremble *huge.* Well over six feet and probably closer to three hundred than two fifty, he and his shoulders seemed to dwarf the wall behind him. Tautly corded arms hung loosely beside a wide, bare chest and a one-, two-, three-, freakin' *four*-rung ladder of ridged abs.

A vee only the truly ripped—or photoshopped—sported cut above his hips, arrowing beneath a tight pair of black football pants that clung to a pair of thick, heavily muscled thighs. Large bare feet she could easily picture smashing small villages were braced almost arrogantly apart. She used to spend hours watching Fred Flintstone powering his prehistoric car with his feet, and that part of the body had never been particularly sexy. Until now.

With a struggle, she shifted her gaze upward, and it snagged on the miles and miles of gorgeous, caramel skin. And not just any caramel. Salted caramel. Rich. Smooth. Honey brown. Yummy. And covered in a palette of ink. Mesmerized by the rich, beautiful art, she inched closer, eager for a closer look.

Bold, black tribals; snarling black panthers; fierce angels with flaming swords; flowing script... The tattoos flowed up his arms, over his shoulders, and across his chest. More beautiful calligraphy ran down the sides of his torso and spanned the bottom of his stomach, disappearing into the low band of his pants.

He was...wow. She had no idea who he was, but he definitely got her vote for sexiest athlete.

She caught a sigh that wormed its way up her throat...or maybe she didn't.

Because his attention shifted away from the photographer in front of him and toward her.

This time, she couldn't hide the swift intake of breath. Was too stunned to try.

Jesus H. Christ.

He was gorgeous.

No, no. That sounded too superficial. Too...shallow. And his face of sharp, defined angles, shadowed hollows, and stark yet patrician lines spoke of strength. The dark hair that dusted his jaw and surrounded the almost lush fullness of his mouth damn near shouted of a carnal sexuality that had heat curling low in her belly like an undulating plume of smoke.

And those eyes.

Amber and green with flecks of gold. An eagle's eyes.

A predator's eyes.

Her heart thudded against her chest and she stiffened her legs. Sprawling out on the floor like a pagan sacrifice eager to be devoured would probably be frowned upon.

Probably.

"Good, you're here. We're ready for you, Giovanna." The photographer lowered his camera and handed it to another person standing behind him.

For a moment, she didn't move. Couldn't move, totally ensnared by the golden gaze that hadn't released her yet. Then, the photographer's words penetrated her lust-dense stupor, and she flinched. Right. He was ready. For Giovanna.

For her.

God, I promise if you get me through this without me embarrassing myself, I'll start attending mass more than twice a year. I'll stop lying to Mama about her arroz con pollo, *and quit thinking evil, homicidal thoughts about Brian... But I'm gonna need you to increase my faith on that last one. I mean, he's a complete douche.*

Oh shit. She mentally slapped a palm to her forehead. Calling her supervisor a douche in a prayer had to at least be a venial sin.

Uncertain whether she had God on her side or not, she forced her mouth into a Giovanna-like smile and stepped forward. Closer to the beautiful Titan.

She risked a peek at him, and once more became instantly ensnared by his intense, multi-hued stare. This close to him and that piercing scrutiny, one thought reverberated in her mind like a foghorn echoing over the Puget Sound...

The gig is up.

No one else had sniffed out the imposter in their midst, but he seemed to peer underneath the makeup, the poofed-and-curled hair, and the skimpy outfit to the gangly, shy, fashion-oblivious nerd beneath. Would he rat her out?

Demand to know who she was in front of everyone? Hell, she'd failed Giovanna even before one click of the camera…

But he remained silent. And more importantly, he shifted that eagle's gaze away from her and back to the photographer.

Relief coursed through her.

But that relief didn't last. Because as she neared the giant in tight pants, her skin pebbled almost to the point of pain. Heat washed over her like a tidal wave, and those tap-dancing nerves erupted into a full-out samba up and down her spine. She didn't have the courage to glance down, but no doubt her nipples were on full display against the flimsy jersey. Damn things.

Stepping close, she gathered the remnants of her rapidly fleeing courage, skipped her gaze up his chest and—was that a *dime* hanging from a thin chain around his neck?—voluntarily met his eyes. "Hi."

Ay Dios mio. Hi? She needed to get out of her office and to the corner bar more often if that was the best she could offer.

"Hello," he replied. "Nice seeing you again, Giovanna."

Molasses—warm, dark, thick. The deep timbre heavy with the flavor of the South slid over her exposed skin like a caress to her senses. She'd never had the pleasure of visiting Louisiana, but she'd bet her DVD of *Sixteen Candles* that sexy drawl came from there.

Then the name he'd called her penetrated. *Giovanna.* But for the first time since embarking upon this ill-conceived farce, excitement spiked with recklessness skipped through her veins.

That's right. She was Giovanna Cruz, confident, gorgeous, and an up-and-coming supermodel. For today at least, Sophia Cruz—antisocial app developer, eighties movie hoarder, DC and Marvel comics geek with a sweets addiction—had been locked away.

Giovanna wouldn't have a problem touching the Titan with the salted caramel skin, eagle eyes, and sun-warmed molasses voice. Wouldn't see an issue with palming those muscular biceps, draping her arms over those wide shoulders, or pressing herself against that hard, big body. Nope. It was part of the job.

And for the next few hours, part of *her* job.

Anticipation and a whole lotta inappropriate lust fluttered in her belly.

Oh hell yes.

Chapter Three

When Zephirin Black left his grandmother's home in New Orleans for college at Louisiana State University ten years ago, she'd sent him off with three pieces of advice.

One. Wrap it up. Josephine Felice Black was too young to have grandbabies.

Two. Go to class and get your education. Josephine Felice Black also didn't raise no dummies.

And three. Whether he had a football in his hand or not, he would always be Josephine Felice Black's oldest grandson. So he'd better act like he had sense, mind his manners, and like the good Lord, don't disrespect her family's name.

She'd doled out other gems along with those main three, but nothing in her seemingly bottomless repertoire had addressed how to conceal a boner when a gorgeous woman pushed up against you during a photo shoot.

Clenching his jaw, Zeph locked down the groan that shoved its way up his throat. With the focus and intensity that had earned him the title of All-Star and Pro Bowl tight end for the Washington Warriors, he concentrated on the whir and click of the photographer's camera. As a six-year veteran in professional football, he had the art of blocking everything out by the goal down. This wasn't his first shoot. It wasn't even his first shoot for *Sports Unlimited*, a magazine that was a cross between *Sports Illustrated* and *Maxim*. Being a popular player for his team and in the league had garnered him endorsements and ad campaigns that had required hours in front of a camera. This was old hat—

Giovanna Cruz arched her back, her head pressing into the crook between his shoulder and neck, the blue, black, and white jersey with his number stretched across the front barely covering her small but firm breasts. Her long, dark hair with its surprising—and sexy as hell—bright blue tips draped across his chest, the strands caressing his skin, the flower and fruit scent teasing his nose. Her fingers splayed across the tops of his thighs, fingertips subtly flexing against him as if testing the muscle. Hell, was she even aware of the little hum she made every time she touched him? And her ass...

Jesus Christ.

He had to think of something, *anything* else besides her ass notched up against his cock.

Frolicking puppies, the smell of the Warriors' locker room after a grueling practice... His last conversation with his grandmother about her "keeping company" with Deacon Bossier and the loud, lascivious snicker that had followed the announcement...

Yeah. That did it. Erection killer.

Slowly relaxing his muscles, he released a low, inaudible breath.

He and his dick were going to have a serious Come to Jesus talk about professionalism.

After hours of organized team activities, or OTAs, his body should've been tired. Even without contact drills, the late June meetings, watching tape, training, and running of basic technique drills still had him yearning for a couch and remote at the end of the day. But energy coursed through him like a live wire, stringing him tight. And he didn't need to risk a glance down to recognize why.

"Do you mind if I try a couple of different poses?" Giovanna asked Gerald, their photographer for the day, her voice a husky, low timbre that reminded him of pure sex. Of the hoarseness that resulted from a goddamn perfect mouth fucking.

His cock twitched behind his pants, obviously agreeing with his mind's train of thought. Gritting his teeth, Zeph forced his body under control. The last thing *Sports Unlimited* or the PTB of the Warriors organization wanted was him on the cover of the magazine sporting wood.

"It's all yours," Gerald replied, momentarily lowering his camera. "Go for it."

Straightening from her pose, she turned to face Zeph. Her teeth worried her full bottom lip, and he clenched his fist to prevent himself from freeing the tender flesh and rubbing his thumb across the lush curve, soothing it. Soothing her. She lifted her chin to meet his gaze with eyes so deep a chocolate brown, he couldn't smother the sudden craving for the rich, strong chicory coffee so popular at home. Dark. Exotic. Beautiful. And if he didn't know any better...uncertain.

Impossible. This wasn't his first time working with Giovanna Cruz, and there were several things he'd call her— stunning, aloof, professional—but uncertain wasn't even included in the top twenty-five. She'd radiated confidence. He frowned, already lifting his hand to cup her hip, ask if something was wrong...

But then she smiled, erasing any hints of insecurity, and his common sense decided to slap the shit out of him with a reality check. This woman had posed for *Maxim* in what could optimistically be called a bathing suit. Whatever he imagined he'd glimpsed must've been a result of lifting too many weights and not drinking enough water.

"Do you mind?" she murmured, shifting so her shoulder pressed into his chest. "Can I get a lift?" She treated him to another small smile. And once again, his apparently delusional mind whispered, "shy," but that was as ridiculous as his "uncertain" observation.

In lieu of answering, he wrapped an arm around her thighs, and bending his knees, hiked her slight weight into the air.

"Thank you for not groaning," she teased, and without questioning where the impulse originated, he released a grunt as if he'd just blocked a three-hundred-pound linebacker from going after his quarterback.

A snicker sounded from above him, and for the first time ever in a photo shoot, he had to fight a smile. That thought sobered him. That and a whole lot of *what the hell?*

Then, he wasn't thinking anything at all.

Not with her arranging her body over his shoulders like a graceful, slinky feline wrapped around her master's neck. He stiffened, shocked but also conscious of granting her all the support she needed with the arm around her thighs and a palm bracing her shoulder. Her movements exhibited no tentativeness, no hesitancy, as if she trusted him not to let any harm come to her. And fuck if that didn't send an inferno of heat whipping through him.

He couldn't see her, but he felt the curve of her hip settle on his left shoulder, and the side of her breast nestled on the opposite shoulder—a fact he actively tried to block out. A slender arm curved under his chin and a hand cupped his cheek. Thick strands of hair tumbled against his face, and he inhaled the scent of the dark, loose curls. In his mind's eye, he could easily picture how the camera would capture them. Her, curled around his shoulders, her head bent forward as if getting ready to take his mouth.

Jesus, this shoot had turned into a torturous, hot-as-hell form of foreplay.

A woman wearing a short black apron with brushes, combs, and other tools tucked into the many pockets rushed onto the set. Holding up a wide-toothed comb, she pinched a lock of Giovanna's hair. "Let me just move this…"

"Leave it," he ordered. The hairstylist froze, blinked. "Please," he added without softening his tone. He wanted her to go away, leave him wrapped in the silken embrace of this woman.

"He's right," Gerald agreed, his camera already clicking away. "Look at me, Giovanna. Beautiful," he praised, closing in for several close-ups before easing away, still shooting. "Got it. Perfect."

A slight tensing of her body telegraphed Giovanna's request to be lowered. For a moment, he tightened his hold on her, and above him, she stilled, as if she sensed the frayed rope that was his control at the moment. Shit. What was wrong with him? After so long in the league, he should be used to beautiful women. Hell, he'd been around this particular woman before, and she hadn't elicited this damn near caveman reaction from him.

Suddenly needing this shoot over—desperate for space— he set her gently on the floor. Her delicate fingers with their bright blue polish dented his skin as she clutched his shoulders for a second too long after he'd released her. And fuck it, a goddamn Tibetan monk couldn't have barred the mental image of those same nails leaving marks on his sweat-dampened skin and flexing back as he drove into tight, hot, wet flesh.

And God knew he wasn't a monk.

Shifting back a step, he placed that much-needed distance between them before he did something deranged and ludicrous like throw her over his shoulder and christen one of these walls.

"Can we try one more?" She turned to Gerald again, and Zeph ground his jaw, surprised he didn't breathe molar dust. Her last request damn near killed him. What now?

"You have this." Gerald waved. "Let's see what you got."

When she pivoted toward Zeph again, took a step toward him, he narrowed his eyes on her, suddenly wary. His muscles tightened, preparing themselves for her touch. For whatever she planned—

She sank to her knees in front of him.

Fuuuuuck.

No way in hell could he have halted the growl that rumbled in his chest and up his throat. Not with her lowering further into a pose that reminded him of Princess Leia at the "feet" of Jabba the Hutt. Except she faced him, her mouth almost level with his cock. Jesus, if he closed his eyes, he could feel her breath on his flesh even through the nylon of his pants. If God suddenly imbued him with the strength of Samson, Zeph still wouldn't have been able to control the blood pumping straight to his cock, filling it. Hardening it. And when she tipped her head back, lifting her gaze to him, he glimpsed that knowledge in those chicory eyes. Noted the gleam of arousal. Fucking drowned in it.

Unconsciously, and without her permission, he threaded his fingers in the thick silk of her hair, gripping it. Tugging it. Tipping her head a little farther back.

He caught the soft gasp of breath that escaped her parted lips. Didn't miss the flutter of her lashes. Or the runaway beating of her pulse within the shallow dip at the base of her throat.

"Damn," someone whispered.

But Zeph didn't glance up. Refused to free her from his regard. Even when Gerald's camera started firing away like the rapid pulses of a disco strobe light. Holding the pose and staring down into her upturned face should've been uncomfortable; it had been in the past. But with every sense attuned to her—the delicate aroma of her perfume or shampoo teasing his nose; the stroke of her hair against the over-sensitized skin of his hand and wrist; the searing press of her breast against his thigh—discomfort didn't register. Just the greedy impulse to open his mouth over that fluttering pulse and set his tongue to it. Set it racing harder.

Only when the photographer instructed her to look at him did he allow her to move. But his hand remained tangled in her curls, the cave dweller part of him he hadn't known existed needing to remind her of his control, of who touched her. Fucking claimed her.

Gone was that gentleman he'd been raised to be. He'd been transformed into this primal being by a woman with sultry eyes, a sex-roughened voice, and a walking wet-dream body.

"I do believe we have everything we need." Gerald beamed at them, handing his camera to an assistant who rushed forward to take the piece of equipment. "Great shoot."

With a sharp nod, Zeph removed his hand from her and just checked himself from curling his fingers into a punishing fist to trap the silken sensation of her hair sliding over his skin. But in a "fuck you" to his resolve not to touch her again, he stretched an arm toward her, that gentleman surging to the forefront again. For a moment, she stared at his palm, then slid hers into his. The touch, wholly innocent, set him on fire. And when he tugged her gently to her feet, he didn't release her.

"Have dinner with me," he said. Ordered. Shit. He hadn't meant to sound so abrasive, but somewhere between her walking onto the set of the photo shoot and her kneeling at his feet, lust had razed his manners to the goddamn ground.

She stared up at him, her scrutiny roaming over his face, and for a long instant, settling on his mouth.

Her gaze jerked back to meet his. "No."

With one lingering survey of him from his beard to his damn bare toes—a survey that smacked of arousal and regret—she pivoted and walked away.

He remained standing on the canvas, watching her disappear behind the white partition.

What the hell just happened?

Chapter Four

"So, I finish training for the day and get in my car. Just as I start it, I see this shadow in my backseat. Turns out, this chick bribed her way past security and onto the lot, and snuck into my car. Nearly scared the shit out of me." Dominic Anderson shook his head, reaching for his beer on the low table he, Zeph, and their three friends surrounded at Doyle's, a bar in Seattle's Pioneer Square that they all often frequented.

"Not literally, I hope," Zeph drawled, tipping his own beer for a long sip.

A middle finger was Dom's only reply.

"You fucked her, didn't you?" Ronin Palamo asked. The star wide receiver for the Warriors narrowed his gaze, propping his elbows on the arms of the chair he sat sprawled in.

"Of course not," Dom objected, outrage darkening his expression.

Zeph damn near rolled his eyes. The only thing missing was a hand clutching proverbial pearls. Dom had recently wrapped up a commercial for a new sneaker line, but his acting skills were hardly good enough to pull off "righteously offended." With that movie-star face, his money, and his career as the Warriors' quarterback, he wasn't a stranger to women throwing themselves at him. The man had to dodge pussy like he juke stepped defense on an all-out blitz.

"She blew him." Tennyson Clark bit into her burger after delivering that bit of insight, an eyebrow raised high. Not only was she Dom's personal assistant, but they had been best friends since they were kids, and when he'd been drafted out of Ohio State, she'd followed him to Seattle. She knew him better than anyone, and that included Zeph and Ronin, who'd played side by side with him these past six years.

"Don't talk with your mouth full," Dom snapped at her.

"That's what he said." Renee Smith, a public relations consultant for the Warriors franchise as well as friend to them all, grinned, wriggling her dark eyebrows like some mustache-twirling, top-hat-wearing cartoon villain.

"I. Said. Nothing. Happened," the quarterback ground out from between clenched teeth.

Ronin snickered. "She *so* blew him."

"Yeah, she did," Renee crowed at the same time.

"Give it up, bruh," Zeph added with a shake of his head.

"Fuckers," Dom growled, glaring at all of them before turning the full power of it on Tennyson, who simply shrugged in return, totally unrepentant. "And you. Snitches get stitches."

"So aside from Dom getting his dick sucked by some random...again...what else is going on? I feel like I haven't seen you guys in forever. Once the season starts, I know it's only going to get worse," Renee lamented, reaching for the other half of Tennyson's burger but receiving a pop on the hand before she could touch it. "Ouch. Damn," she grumbled. "Anyway, Zeph, wasn't your photo shoot for *Sports Unlimited* today?"

"Yeah," he said, leaving it at that.

"You might've said 'yeah,' but that tone was all Get Outta My Shit." Ronin laughed, leaning forward and propping his elbows on his thighs. "I talked to Jason earlier, and that asshole didn't mention anything. What happened?"

For a moment, a pall hung over their small area, the lively din of the pub fading a little under the weight of the silence. Ronin winced, while Tennyson ducked her head, and a tic set up along the line of Dom's jaw.

Jason Wilder, the last member of their tight circle, and Renee and Ronin had all grown up together in the Seattle area. But after Jason and Renee hooked up months ago, the friendship had imploded right after the sex ended. Now all of them resembled a fractured family more than a close-knit group. Due to the bitterness between the two, all of them hadn't been able to hang together in months; it was either Renee or Jason, but never the two together.

Shit, sometimes it seemed like they were caught in a custody battle.

"Because there was nothing to tell," Zeph said into the tense, awkward quiet. "It's not like it was the first time we worked together." He narrowed his eyes on Ronin over the rim of his bottle. "I swear, bruh. You and gossip. Makes me want to check you for panties instead of shorts."

Ronin took a deep gulp of his Guinness and wiped the back of his hand across his mouth. And women still found him irresistible. Must be the lumberjack look with the long hair and full beard, 'cause it definitely couldn't be the manners.

"Shows how much you know," Ronin said, jabbing his mug in Zeph's direction. "I'm straight free-balling it."

"Oh eeew." Renee wrapped both hands around her throat, gagging.

"Those aren't the jeans you 'borrowed' and never gave back, are they?" Dom demanded, glaring at his friend.

"Quarterback, you *wish* you needed this much room," Ronin drawled.

"While I'm choosing to overlook your sexist remark about gossip and women," Tennyson interjected, her even tone like a cool, calm lake amidst the loud overlapping back and forth, "I would like to point out that the lady under discussion is over at the bar. Has been for the last hour."

Zeph's head jerked up, and, almost against his will, he searched the long length of the bar on the other side of the room. There. At the far end. That blue sky-tipped dark hair, coffee and cream skin, and vixen body were unmistakable. Giovanna Cruz.

The bite of her rejection still prickled under his skin like the stinger of a bee. Especially when he'd been so sure it'd been attraction he'd read in her eyes, in her body. No, he wasn't the manwhore Ronin and Dom were, but in the ten years since he'd entered college, he'd had his fair share of women. He could easily decipher between pretending and real arousal. Even his ex Shalene, who'd been after the fame of being a WAG, had enjoyed the sex. Hell, in the sheets might've been the only place she hadn't lied.

So yeah, Giovanna had wanted him. But she'd still turned him down and walked away without a backward glance, leaving him trying to talk down a raging hard-on in nylon pants.

A hard-on that had already risen to half-mast with just a brief sighting of her.

"Oh suuure," Renee said from beside him. "I'm totally convinced nothing happened now."

But he didn't reply to her smart-ass comment. Didn't even say bye to his friends. He was already on his feet, striding across the floor.

Lust swirled through his veins, thick and hot. A voice whispered he was making a huge fucking mistake. All of his focus should be centered on the upcoming season and winning. Not to mention he'd been in this place before. Different woman, different face, but same situation. And he'd paid the price. It'd made him wary of those who lived their lives in "the business." From his experience, fame was a narcotic that could never satisfy some people.

So pursuing this...this *thing* with Giovanna the up-and-coming cover model could boomerang to bite him on the ass.

Yet, he still continued to wind his way around tables and people with unerring accuracy. He was a guided missile locked on his target, and nothing was getting in his way.

• • •

"Thanks." Sophia smiled at the bartender as the woman set a napkin and another Lemondrop—her third—on the bar top in front of her.

"Umm, sweetie, you might want to slow down. Those things are delicious as hell, but they can sneak up on you. Last time I tangled with one, I ended up on the bathroom floor," Delia, the hairstylist from the day's shoot, warned.

"Oh pooh." Mona, the makeup artist, flicked her fingers in the direction of the lemonade-flavored cocktail. Or as Sophia liked to call it, shiny-happy-feelings-in-a-glass. "Remember, the tattoo. She's had man trouble. She deserves this. Drink up, honey."

Instead of disabusing Mona of her assumption about Sophia's reason for her ink, she took a long, deep sip of the alcohol. And hummed at the cold, lemony goodness as it slid down her throat. Damn, that was good.

When the two women had invited her out after the shoot, Sophia had almost turned them down. Pretending to be her model twin had been exhausting, and the reasonable part of her asserted that the longer she continued the charade, the bigger the chance of slipping and blowing her cover. But the side that quietly enjoyed the attention she'd received today—the side that she didn't need a therapist to tell her was firmly rooted in that sixteen-year-old high-school girl—had jumped at the opportunity. For a night—a Thursday night, at that—she would hang with new friends, laugh, have fun. They'd already introduced her to Lemondrops. And if the women thought they were hanging with...not Sophia, well, she'd try and forget that for the next few hours.

"We should so find you a man. The best way to get over one is to get under another," Delia said, running a fingertip around her sugar-rimmed glass. "This bar is a popular place. All the local celebrities come here. Including"—she gave a full-body shiver as she sucked her fingertip into her mouth—"football players."

"Yeah." Mona sighed. "Those huge bodies, tight abs, big ol' thighs and...hands." She snickered, then, without warning, she seized both Delia and Sophia by the wrists. "Oh shit, look who's sitting over there by the back window." When they went to turn on their barstools, her grip tightened. "Don't be so obvious!" she hissed. "Nice 'n' slow. It's Dominic Anderson and Ronin Palamo." A wicked smile curved her purple-tinted lips. "And your guy, Zephirin Black."

The light buzz from the cocktails she'd inhaled evaporated like fizz in a flat soda. A gale of roughly one-hundred miles per hour whipped and roared between her ears, her heart adding the bass of thunder.

Zephirin here. In the same bar. Feet away.

Oh shit.

Earlier, she'd refused his dinner invitation. But that had been a matter of self-preservation. During the photo shoot, the hot-sex-on-a-platter football player had shaken her. Rendered her damn near speechless and definitely thoughtless. And for someone who had a cover story to maintain, that blared danger... *He* blared danger. Big, neon red, don't-fucking-try-it danger.

Delia and Mona were one thing, but holding her own *alone* with Zephirin, with those eagle eyes focused on her for several hours? Yeah, she didn't trust herself. She'd been right to turn him down. To walk away. End it so she didn't burrow deeper into a lie.

Now if only her nipples and va-jay-jay would just get the notice, she could return to her night of drinking. Any minute now...

"Holy shit. Zeph's headed this way," Delia squealed, twisting back around on her barstool, eyes wide. "Oh Jesus. I can get pregnant just from hearing that man talk." Taking a huge gulp of her margarita, she fluttered a hand next to her face.

While the other two women pretended to not see the huge mountain of manflesh striding their way, Sophia couldn't tear her gaze off of him. She couldn't look away from the stare that seemed to pin her to the backless seat.

Zephirin Black. Even his name was sexy as hell.

Twenty-eight years old. Six feet, six inches, two hundred and eighty-three pounds. Hailed from New Orleans, Louisiana. Attended Louisiana State University where he'd been a star tight end for the Tigers all four years, and was key in leading them to two SEC championships. Graduated with a Bachelor's in finance, and drafted to the Washington Warriors six years ago. All Pro every year, Offensive MVP once.

Wikipedia was a wonderful thing. But it hadn't mentioned diddly about his thighs possessing the size and strength of tree trunks. Or that when he lifted a woman, his hands easily spanned her waist and made her feel like a Sherman tank could be headed straight for her and she'd still have no fear of being harmed. Or that under the hot gleam of lights, his skin resonated an intoxicating, sensual musk of sunshine and sex.

Nope. Epic fail, Wikipedia.

Maybe if her brain stopped insisting on replaying moments from the photo shoot, then she could do something other than gawk like a completely starstruck groupie. Like, if she could forget the greedy need that had ripped through her when she knelt at his feet, her mouth inches from the surely-those-are-socks-in-there bulge straining against the laces of his football pants. Or if she could somehow erase the slight but delicious sting of her scalp when he'd tugged on her hair… tilting her head back…as if positioning her for…

Christ. She picked up her glass and, following Delia's lead, sipped long and deep. Liquid courage was a must.

Seconds slowed to the pace of years, but eventually he approached, stopping directly in front of her. His eyes appeared even more piercing under the dim bar lighting, the green almost eclipsed by the gold. Everything in her vibrated and hummed. The light purple tank top and flowing white skirt she'd worn had seemed adequate for a night out, but under his perusal, she felt stripped. Naked.

"Ladies," Zephirin greeted all of them, even though he never removed his stare from her.

Mona and Delia's voices tripped over one another as they replied, their giddiness and pleasure a palpable thing.

"Would you two mind if I spoke with Giovanna for a moment?" He dipped his chin in the direction from where he'd come. "I'll switch places with you."

She wouldn't have been surprised if a cloud of exhaust had plumed behind her newfound friends as they abandoned her to zoom across the room and socialize with Zephirin's circle. Son of a bitch. Hadn't they ever heard of "bros before hoes?" Or however that would go with women. Chicks before dicks, that's what it was.

"Giovanna." The aforementioned pregnancy-inducing

drawl caressed her name—or rather her twin's name—as he lowered onto the nearest stool. "It's nice seeing you again."

"You, too," she said, swigging down more of the cocktail.

"You okay?" he asked, leaning a bent elbow on the bar top. The move brought him a scant inch closer. Forcing her to imbibe even more.

"Sure. Why do you ask?"

A beat of silence. "Because you're sucking down that drink like it's about to run away screaming."

The snicker escaped her before she could trap it, the crackling dry tone and joking unexpected. He'd done the same—caught her off guard—when he'd unexpectedly teased her during the shoot. Even now, he seemed so…intense. Stoic. And his demeanor had her caught between a nervous urge to babble and a need to… Hell, just a need.

"Here you go." The bartender appeared, setting a tall glass down in front of Sophia even though she hadn't ordered another. Oh well, hers was just about halfway gone, so yay, more alcohol. "How 'bout you, Mr. Black?" she fairly purred, crossing her arms on the bar, leaning over and placing her admittedly impressive cleavage on full display. "Can I get you something?"

"Something" not being anything on the menu. Unless they'd suddenly added pussy al dente on the entree list.

Wow. Sophia peered down into her glass. Alcohol must bring out her bitchy side.

But really, how could Sophia blame her? The man, with his stylish cap, black shirt that covered his shoulders and wide chest like a shameless hussy, and perfectly tailored gray pants, was gorgeous eye candy all by himself. With a face and body like that, millions of dollars and fame just seemed like overkill.

Zephirin placed his order for another beer then glanced at Sophia. "Giovanna? Would you like something else?" Her belly did that involuntary stop-drop-and-roll thing at the sound of his deep, honeyed accent. But underneath, an oily unease and...jealousy crawled. She hated that he called her by someone else's name. No, not just someone's. Her sister's.

Inhaling, she deliberately squelched both the fire drill motions and the disquiet. "Yes, sure." She grabbed one of the menus resting several inches in front of her. After a quick scan, she said, "I'll have the steak burger, medium rare and fully loaded, with a side of garlic truffle fries. Make it a large order," she recited, already tasting the butter and salty goodness in her mouth. The alcohol should've filled her stomach, but she was suddenly hungry. Giving the behemoth of a man next to her side eye, she amended that hungry to ravenous.

Zephirin arched an eyebrow, and an anvil labeled "Oh shit!" plummeted out of the sky and slammed on top of her. A working model didn't eat big-ass burgers piled with everything from lettuce to onion rings. One damn sure didn't request a double order of fries.

"I'll have the same." He nodded to the bartender.

"Sounds great," the other woman cooed. "Is there anything else you need? A refill of your water? Lemon and lime, right? Would you like bread while you wait for your entrée?"

Sophia barely contained a snort as he turned down the waitress's offer of "whatever he wanted," sending her away with a disappointed pout but an extra sway in her hips. Shaking her head, Sophia glanced at Zephirin, and the breath she'd just sucked in moments earlier evaporated like smoke in her lungs. Those eyes. She couldn't get used to them—or their power to render her mute. And dumb. And horny.

Desperately, she scrambled for a safe topic. Nothing that had anything to do with today's shoot, her mouth being anywhere near his cock, or her nipples currently trying to drill holes through her top. And definitely nothing about her identity.

"So, those are your friends, huh? I'm getting a real *Breakfast Club* vibe off of you... No, wait. Scratch that. *St. Elmo's Fire*. Definitely *St. Elmo's Fire*. The brunette is definitely giving me Jules. The killer stilettos scream party girl. And the lumberjack? Kirby sans long hair. Oh, and the one with the pretty curls? Wendy. Especially since she can't keep her eyes off the Sam Heughan look-alike. So that would make him Billy since Wendy's obviously in love with him. That leaves Kevin, Alec, and Leslie..." Her voice trailed off as the words she'd just rambled replayed through her head. *Oh fuck*. Somebody stop her mouth. Or better yet, hit her with an elephant tranquilizer and put her ass out. She cleared her throat. "I'm sor—"

"Our other friend, Jason, would be Alec. He's a twenty-first century yuppie," Zephirin added, interrupting her apology.

Sophia blinked. Stared. Blinked some more. "You know *St. Elmo's Fire*?" she asked, disbelief rife in her voice. Aside from Giovanna, no one knew *St. Elmo's Fire*.

He shrugged one of his massive shoulders. "My younger sister was a Blockbuster junkie when we were kids. It was one of her favorite movies. I might've watched it a time...or ten." He snorted. "Not that I had much of a choice."

She laughed at the mental image of a girl who shared his beautiful features forcing him to sit in front of a television and making his much younger self watch the eighties movie.

"By process of elimination that leaves Kevin," he continued, but she shook her head.

"You have that broody thing going on, but nothing else. Unless you're secretly in love with your best friend's girlfriend." Heat soared up her neck and into her face. "I mean, maybe...uh..."

"Are you trying to ask me if I'm in love with someone?" He leaned farther onto the bar, his feet parted firmly on the floor, his long legs sprawled out on either side of her stool. A stool that obviously hadn't been fashioned for six-foot-six giants.

"No," she stammered. "Of course not." She lifted her half-empty glass to her lips. Sipped. "So, are you?"

Though his full mouth remained in a straight line, humor seemed to flicker in his eyes. "No," he replied softly. Then in a slightly harder voice, "Are you?"

"No," she whispered.

A beat of tense silence pulsed between them. It lasted for a second, but it was filled with a thick heat that wrapped itself around her, infiltrated her, set her veins on fire. It might've been smothering if not for the arousal...the need weighing it down.

"You're different," he said, smashing the hush like a sledgehammer taken to a plaster wall.

"How so?" she asked, forcing a calm into her voice that had ceased to exist from the moment she'd stood in that studio and laid eyes on him for the first time.

Again, her nerves started jackhammering away under her skin. She always felt on the verge of discovery with him, as if any second he would call her out as the liar she was. And then she would have to go old school "You can't handle the truth!" Jack Nicholson on him.

Hmm. Maybe the Lemondrops were starting to work their magic.

"There's the food order, for one."

Hell. Another sip of alcohol. "A girl's gotta eat."

"Then there's the tattoo." His intense scrutiny dipped toward her waist, setting off sparks and crackles below the area. With just one look. If he ever got his hands on her—inside her—she'd probably self-combust. But damn, wouldn't she die happy? "Not many mainstream models wear ink on their skin. It's beautiful," he murmured. "Does it have special meaning?"

Special meaning. More of a reminder. Of a time when she'd been mercilessly bullied and tormented daily. Though they were twins, Giovanna had been popular, accepted; she'd belonged. And Sophia, the heavier twin with her dyed hair, quirky clothing, shyness, and 122 IQ score, hadn't. Giovanna had tried her best to defend her, but she couldn't always.

Not until Sophia had entered college had she started to come into her own. And accept herself. Love herself.

The tattoo was a testament to both her past and present.

But she could say none of that to him. Even if she were sitting across from him as Sophia instead of Giovanna, unloading all of her baggage on him had to be on the "101 Ways to Turn Off a Man" list in the Dating Guidebook.

"It's pretty," she said with a patented "Giovanna Cruz" smile. "Sorry to disappoint. What about yours?" Images of his inked body scrolled across her brain like a parade float dedicated to complete bad-boy sexiness. Clearing her throat, she gestured toward his chest with her glass. "Does the panther have special meaning?"

He studied her, the long fingers of one hand splayed over his muscular thigh. "Yes," he said into the brief moment of silence. "It's for my grandmother. She raised my sister and me. The panther is a symbol of courage, power, and grace. That's her."

Obvious love for his grandmother resonated in his low, molasses timbre as well as the open, honest words. Not many men of her acquaintance would've waxed poetic about a parent in fear of appearing like a mama's boy or soft. But not Zephirin. She didn't think it was possible, but somehow it made him that much sexier.

"Now I feel totally shallow," she muttered.

He shook his head. "No, not shallow," he contradicted. "Just not exactly truthful." Before her heart could lodge itself in her throat, he added, "About the tattoo. But it's okay if you don't want to share. I'm patient."

Sophia snorted, hiding behind nonchalance when inside she melted and shrank from his piercing perception. "I'm pretty sure calling your date a liar is a surefire way of blowing your chances at another one," she said, voice wry. Then, her statement replayed through her mind and slapped her in the face. *Hard.* "Not that this is a date or anything," she rushed to add, the words running up on one another so fast they sounded more like, "Notthatthisadateoranything."

"And there's another difference," he observed, cocking his head to the side. "You were more"—he paused—"reserved the first time we worked together."

Oh damn. Had he asked Giovanna out, and she'd turned him down?

She struggled to maintain her composure as the horrifying thought raced across her mind. Her twin had never mentioned him, but then why would she? Being hit on by the men she met in the industry was probably part of the job description. The greasy slide of envy returned, this time thicker, darker, harder to erase. Jealousy of the obvious attraction Zephirin was giving her. Only because he believed she was Giovanna. Which, at the moment, was Sophia. But if he'd met Sophia *as* Sophia, he'd never have been interested.

Briefly she closed her eyes, the urge to escape thudding in her chest and head like a primal drum. But the desire to steal this date—this night—with this man even if it was based on a lie throbbed harder, louder.

But her reasons for turning down his invite to dinner earlier hadn't suddenly evaporated—he believed her to be someone else. And not just anyone, but her twin sister. The pretense during the shoot was one thing, but carrying on the act outside of it was lying. If she were smart, she would get her burger and fries to go, tell Zephirin good-bye, and leave for her quiet, empty home.

But like some geeky, lust-filled version of Cinderella—and with a little help from the alcohol lubricating her inhibitions—she just wanted to be someone else for a little while. Enjoy this dance of attraction, savor the sensual gleam in his eyes, for the next few hours before she returned to her normal life of codes, cramped offices, shitty bosses, and thrift store jeans. Just one night to be someone different—someone who sexy-as-sin football players found attractive. Was that so bad? To seize this moment for herself since she would never see him again after tonight?

"I could've been having an off day then," she offered the vague explanation with a shrug. "I don't really remember. I'm sorry."

"What are you apologizing for?" He arched that eyebrow again. She really shouldn't find that so insanely hot.

Another shrug of a shoulder. "If I hurt your feelings."

Surprise flashed in his eagle eyes before they narrowed on her. "You're serious, aren't you?"

I'm so out of my element here. And no good at this. Floundering, she fumbled for and wrapped her fingers around her refreshed drink, the cold condensation chilling her skin. "Of course." She frowned. "Is something wrong?"

For a long second, he didn't reply. "No, sorry. I'm just not used to people apologizing for anything. Being genuine. Even less accustomed to that kind of honesty." For a moment, something dark moved in his eyes. "I've been lied to so often, the truth is my white whale."

Uneasiness pitched and rocked in her stomach because she was one more person he could count as a deceiver. *"Para decir mentiras y comer pescado hay que tener mucho cuidado,"* she murmured. When he cocked his head to the side, she explained, "It's an old saying my mother used to say all the time when I was younger. It means, 'When lying and eating fish, one must be very careful.' Like when eating fish with bones, you have to be very careful telling lies because people can get seriously hurt by them."

A heartbeat of silence passed. "Your mother seems like a very smart woman," he finally said.

"So she's fond of telling me," Sophia whispered.

Then he loosed a soft, gruff burst of laughter, a half smile quirking a corner of his sensual mouth.

"That's beautiful." The admission stumbled off her tongue before she could trap it, lock it up, and throw the damn key into the fiery pits of Mount Doom. Maybe he hadn't heard—

"What is?"

Fucking Lemondrops. Swallowing a sigh, she waved her hand in the vicinity of his face. "Your smile. And laugh. First time I've seen either. They're..."

"Beautiful," he supplied when her voice trailed off.

"Yes." Well, hell. Where was a marauding army of orcs when you needed one? *Jesus.* This was exactly why she didn't play this dating game. She didn't know the rules, and ultimately ended up violating them in all manner of socially awkward ways.

"Who are you?" The hard, rough murmur caught her off guard almost as much as the question.

Her heart thudded against her rib cage. "I—" She swallowed. Tried again. "I don't know what you mean."

Once more, he leaned forward, this time eliminating all personal space. Both hands palmed his thighs, and his face hovered inches from hers. A tingle started prickling at the back of her neck. A warning of danger. If she owned one ounce of common sense, she would blurt out some excuse and leave. But her ass remained planted in the chair even though the ominous sense that she was in way over her head tripped down her spine.

"I want to know who you are. The guarded, untouchable model from a year ago who could freeze a man's balls off, or the woman from today who sat at my feet, teasing my cock with her mouth? Which one is the lie?" His voice deepened, lowered so the words seemed to travel over gravel before coming out of his mouth. "You both have the same dark, damn near bottomless eyes, the same gorgeous body, and golden skin that makes a man dream of marking it with his tongue and hands. But this woman wears ink on her skin and piercings in her mouth and eyebrow."

Stunned, she lifted a hand to her bottom lip, brushing a fingertip across the spot where the small hoop she'd removed for the shoot would've normally been. With the dark red lipstick, the tiny hole shouldn't have been visible. How had he...?

He emitted a sound that seemed caught between a huff of laughter and a soft *tsk*. "You have a mouth made for sex. You think I wouldn't notice everything about it?"

Mouth made for sex. Made for sex. Sex. Sex.

Ay bandito. The words echoed in her head like roars in the stadium where he played. They resonated in her chest, her belly...vibrated between her legs.

Her empty core clenched and spasmed around those words.

Maybe he glimpsed the heat setting her flesh on fire in her face. Or heard it in the almost inaudible whimper she didn't quite manage to stifle.

Either way, something hot and bright flared in his eyes. "Look down at the bar. Out the window. Anywhere but at me," he growled.

"Why?" she breathed, not removing her stare from the face that had gone taut with lust. It didn't matter that she'd never glimpsed this expression on a man's face before. She recognized it on *him*.

"Because those gorgeous eyes are practically begging me to..." He trailed off, a muscle ticking along his clenched jaw. Part of her wished he'd finished the thought. That same part almost demanded he tell her. "Giovanna—"

"Sophia. Call me Sophia," she interrupted, unable to bear hearing him call her by her twin's name again. She needed to hear *her* name uttered in that sex-and-sin voice. At least once.

"What?" He frowned.

"It's my middle name," she blurted, the lie burning like wildfire on her tongue. A second of *damn* bombarded her. She was playing with fire, giving him her real name—asking that he use it. He could google her as easily as she'd searched him. Although, given the number of Sophia Cruzes in the United States alone—and that she was one of millions of app developers and not a model or football star—he probably wouldn't find her name a top hit. And she'd asked Giovanna to keep her out of her publicity bios, just for privacy reasons. Working in the tech industry made one paranoid like that.

Still, it was a risky if not foolish move...

But damn if she would take it back. Not if it meant having that drawl rolling around her real name. "Giovanna is the model. Sophia is..." Her voice disappeared, the breath stuttering in her throat. "Sophia is the woman you described. The woman whose eyes are begging you to..." She let the sentence dangle just as he had. So he would fill in the blank.

The words whispered between them, barely loud enough to be heard. But he caught them. The tightening of his solid jaw underneath the shadow of his beard telegraphed that he'd caught them.

"Are you drunk?"

She blinked. It took a moment for the half question, half

demand to register. Where had that come from? "Excuse me?"

"Are. You. Drunk?" he gritted out.

"No." She did an internal check. Feeling good and a little warm, but definitely not drunk. "No. Why?"

"Because I want to make sure this is Giovanna—or Sophia—talking and not the Lemondrops."

In spite of the need carving a hole inside her, a short bark of laughter erupted from her. "I appreciate you checking, but no."

He reached out, cupped her jaw in his big palm. A shudder rippled through her, and she clenched her thighs tight in an attempt to trap and alleviate the sweet, pulsing ache there. His thumb pressed into the corner of her bottom lip, directly over the pierced hole. He didn't seem to care that her lipstick would stain his finger. Didn't seem to mind getting messy. And damn if that wasn't some kind of hot.

"Sophia," he murmured. "Pretty. Sweet...and sexy as hell."

In an abrupt motion, he leaned back, taking his touch with him. His fingers, including the lipstick-smudged thumb, curled into a fist on his thigh. Tension seemed to emanate from his big body, the casual sprawl on the stool abandoned for a posture so straight, so still, he reminded her of that dark predator on his chest.

"Your food should be here very shortly," the bartender announced, her appearance catching Sophia by surprise. She'd been so caught up in Zephirin—in his bright, heated gaze—that she hadn't even noticed the other woman's arrival. "Can I refill your drinks?"

"I need the check," Zephirin said, not releasing Sophia from his visual snare. "And please box up the dinners."

"Uh...um...okay." The other woman cleared her throat. "I'll be right back."

A part of Sophia acknowledged that she should be mortified at his instructions. Maria Von Trapp's Mother Superior could've guessed why he'd suddenly requested the check. Still, embarrassment hadn't sent fire hurtling through her. Lust claimed that responsibility. And the minutes until the bartender returned with the tab and a paper bag with their boxed dinners seemed to crawl and race by at the same time. By the time Zephirin stood, his wide palm at the small of her back, and guided her from the pub, her nerves, strung so tight, wept for mercy.

Ohmigod, I'm doing this. I'm going to have sex with Zephirin Black.

Air whistled in her head, her ears having transformed into a wind tunnel for her shallow breaths. Her heart provided the bursts of thunder underneath.

"Wait," she said.

Even though it'd been barely above a whisper, he must've heard her plea because he abruptly halted as if a barrier had sprung up in front of him. With a dexterity that she could easily picture him using on the field, he maneuvered her out of the flow of pedestrian traffic and back up against the brick wall of an adjacent antique shop that had closed for the evening.

He didn't touch her, instead slid his hands into the front pockets of his pants. Following his lead, she tucked hers behind her. If she dared to touch him, they might get arrested for indecent exposure.

"Changing your mind?" he asked.

Changing her mind? God, no. Even though, to be fair to him, she should walk away. Let this go. Already, guilt squirmed under the arousal and need that damn near consumed her. This wasn't her; her determination to be true and honest to herself had been one of the reasons she'd suffered so much grief in her life.

She didn't lie, didn't play games.

Yet, if she revealed her identity to him right now, Zephirin would walk away. She harbored no doubt about that. Not when the memory of his comment about lies, spoken in that hard, flat voice, flickered in her head, along with the dark emotion that had shadowed his eyes. He would feel duped, played a fool. Possibly even reveal what she and Giovanna had done to *Sports Unlimited*. Telling the truth would risk harming her sister's career.

That's not your primary motivation. Admit it.

Sophia squeezed her eyes closed, as if the motion could also shut out the nagging, smug voice of her conscience. Yes, she loved her sister—had taken part in this ridiculous charade to help her. But first and foremost in her mind was the need coursing through her veins demanding to be satisfied. How many times had anyone spoken to her the way Zephirin had? Raw. Dirty. Almost desperate. How many times had a man who probably starred in hundreds of thousands of women's fantasies ever given her a second glance, much less stared at her like he would lose his shit if he wasn't inside her in the next five-point-two seconds? How many times had she just taken something for herself?

Zero. To all questions.

As long as she could remember, she'd been the "other" twin. And that was one of the kinder references. She'd been called plainer, smarter—a euphemism for unattractive—and in high school, fugly. Those four years had done a number on her self-esteem, but over time, she'd found her niche with computers, and as a result, had gained confidence in that area. Yet inside, she still felt like "Giovanna's sister." The one who always lost when it came to comparisons against the gorgeous, vivacious model. The one who would never be quite...enough.

But tonight... Tonight, she was the beautiful twin. The

twin who incited that heat in Zephirin's eyes. Yes, he believed she was Giovanna, but it was her who had this gorgeous man's body strung tight with tension.

It probably made her a selfish bitch, but she couldn't push him away. She wanted this night. This memory.

"No," she finally answered, lifting her lashes. "I just have a...condition." Exhaling a breath, she didn't wait for him to reply, but rushed ahead. "One night. This"—she waved a hand in the scant space between their chests—"can only last for tonight."

He remained silent for so long, she feared he would call it off, walk away. A muscle ticked along his clenched jaw, his body a living wall emanating enough heat to battle the June night.

"Where do you live?" he growled.

"Alaska Junction."

"My apartment's downtown. Quicker. Let's go." In spite of the harshness of his voice, his grip when he folded his fingers around her upper arm was gentle. But firm. And both stole her breath, kindled a ball of heat deep inside her. Because in that moment, she had a flash of foresight about how he would take her. Tender. In control. Soft, but with a power, intensity, and fierceness that would render her his to do whatever he wished.

She shivered.

Game on.

Chapter Five

Apartment.

He'd called this high-rise condo with unobstructed views of the Elliott Bay waterfront, Mt. Rainier, and the glittering, alive Seattle skyline at exclusive One Pacific Tower an apartment.

Sophia gaped at the cathedral ceiling with its mural of mosaic tiles and exotic stone that soared over a huge living and dining area. Freestanding walls sectioned off rooms, but she could easily peek into the cavernous spaces with their marble fireplaces, furniture straight out of *Harper's Bazaar Interiors*, and floor-to-ceiling windows of immaculately clean glass.

Christ on the Cross, so this was how the other half lived.

She didn't think anything could eclipse the desire that had been riding her for the ten-minute drive and the elevator ride here. But shock at his obvious wealth had definitely quieted some of it.

"Nice place," she complimented, striving for nonchalance instead of astonishment. A model, even of Giovanna's up-and-coming status, would be used to such displays of affluence. She'd shared about the parties of clients she'd attended with Sophia countless times.

A hard chest pressed against her back, and the arousal she'd believed banked to embers flared to roaring life as if he'd flicked a Bic lighter inside her. And when the heavy thickness of an erection nudged her ass and lower back, her knees almost buckled under the flood of need that swamped her.

Up until now, Zephirin had kept a small but definite distance between them. But, with the door to his home closed to all prying eyes, he'd obviously decided he no longer had to maintain that space. He palmed her hips just like the football he was paid millions to catch and carry. Why that thought should send another blast of heat spiraling through her, she couldn't explain. Hell, at this moment she couldn't have told someone her name. Not when he'd lowered his head, his lush, carnal mouth grazing her cheekbone.

"I can give you a tour," he murmured, his fingers opening over her lower belly. "Or I can take you to the bedroom and bury my face between your legs. Your choice."

A whimper of pure, grade-A lust clawed its way free of her throat.

"Bedroom," she breathed. "Definitely the bedroom."

She felt, not saw, that quirk of his lips against her skin. "One thing first."

Before she could lodge a complaint, his hand closed around her throat in an embrace that thrilled her with its dominance. In no way did it restrict her breathing—quite the opposite. The sexual hold caused the air to burst from her lungs in rapid-fire succession. His thumb nudged her chin, tilting her head back. And then, she didn't have a need for breath. Because he gave her his own.

His mouth covered hers, claiming it. Taking it. Helpless

to the onslaught of desire that surged within her, she parted her lips on the edge of a hungry moan. She was powerless to hold any response back from him—she wouldn't have even if she could. Tonight was for freedom from inhibition. To indulge in every sinful, not-good-for-you thing that her mind had ever conjured in the darkest hours of night. And his touch, his mouth—this man—was all that and then some.

When he thrust his tongue between her lips, she opened wider for him, twisting hers around his, dueling, dancing, giving. He tipped her head back farther until she rested on his solid shoulder, and tilting his, slanted his mouth over hers. Taking a deeper kiss, licking, sucking, leaving no area of her undiscovered. If a kiss could be deemed sex, she considered herself well and truly fucked.

And yet, she still needed more.

Breaking his erotic hold on her neck with some regret, she turned, balling her fingers in his shirt and arching up on her tiptoes to deepen the kiss. To taste more of him, all he had to give—and then demand more. What she couldn't put into words, she voiced with her tongue, her lips, her moans, the restless, almost frantic clench and release of her fingers.

With a growl that rumbled in his chest and over her breasts, he cupped her face, taking what she freely offered, until all she could do was gasp and tremble. When those big hands slid down over her shoulders, her knees buckled as if his hold had been the only thing keeping her up. But he was right there, catching her. In a show of casual strength that left her even more breathless, he hiked her up, palming her ass and bracing her until she locked her legs around his waist.

God. Lust rippled through her, and she tucked her head beneath his jaw, as if she could hide from the power of it. From the rock-hard length of him notched against that empty, aching, wet part of her. Of course, a man his size would have a cock equally large. But...damn. A faint voice in the back of her head whispered a panicky, "How in the hell is that supposed to fit?" But a more vociferous one drowned it out, yelling, "Who cares? As long as it gets inside." The rest of her body, and her apparent whore of a vagina, agreed.

Tightening her arms around his neck, she opened her mouth over his neck, sampled the salted caramel skin, hummed as his sweet musk melted on her tongue like the candy his skin reminded her of. And her hips—with a mind of their own—ground against that awe-inspiring erection like her sex was trying to give it a stamp of approval.

"Fuck," he muttered, his head falling back, granting her lips and tongue easier access, his fingers flexing over her ass.

Taking that as a sign of appreciation, she rolled her hips again, using him as leverage. Once more, she bucked against that delicious length, a half cry, half whimper catching in her throat with each grind over her clit and folds, the thin material of her skirt a laughable barrier. She shuddered, a wicked heat sliding through her, settling on the quivering flesh between her thighs.

"Jesus," she gasped, tilting her head back and rubbing over him in complete abandon. And he stood there, supporting her with his strength, allowing her to use his body to get off. And that craved for, but often elusive, release glimmered on the horizon behind her closed lids. So near, but... A whimper escaped her, and she dug her nails into the nape of his neck, clutching him as she tried to get closer. Tried to push herself over that edge...

"You need help getting there, baby?" he asked, already striding from the room, but not going far. In seconds, her back met a wall in a corridor, his body pressed between her spread legs keeping her in place.

He flattened a palm above her head, the other sliding up her calf, knee, and thigh, dragging her skirt with it. Air brushed over her exposed skin, grazing the damp panel of her panties. A part of her acknowledged that she should be at least a little embarrassed over the state of her underwear, and having his gaze pinned there. But that part disintegrated under the sweep of his thumb over the tender, sensitive flesh bordering the drenched cotton. That part gave way like a soaked paper bag under the graze of his nail over her swollen folds.

"You need me to take the edge off?" he offered, lifting his head.

What did he see there? Desperation? Frustration? A need that twisted her up in so many knots on the inside she must resemble a snarled ball of thread.

"Do it," she begged. "I want..." She arched her back, unable to string the words together detailing what she desired, that embarrassment rearing its ugly head in spite of the arousal careening through her veins like a wild thing.

"I know what you want," he assured her with that deep, sexy drawl that contained the sultry South. "This isn't going to take long, is it?" Once more, his stare shifted down to her sex.

She didn't think he required an answer, but she gave him one anyway. "No," she whispered with a shake of her head. She hungered for him with a passion that should've had alarms blaring in her head, but nothing mattered except his touch. Except release.

He lowered his head and took her mouth, thrusting his tongue between her lips.

Just as he drove his fingers into her body.

She screamed.

Splintered.

Into pieces.

Tearing her mouth from his, she loosed another cry as he crooked his fingers, rubbing at a patch high up in her sex. Even before the world realigned, it was cracking apart again.

"That's it. That's it, baby," he growled the dark encouragement into her ear, his molasses drawl changing the word to *bae-beh*. God, it was sexy. As hot as his teeth scraping the curve of her ear. "All yours."

Trembling, she clung to his shoulders, her hips still riding his hand, chasing the aftershocks that continued to ripple through her.

"Goddamn, you're beautiful," he praised, claiming another kiss from her. Still weak from the best orgasm of her life, she didn't utter a word as he whirled around, cradling her against his chest, and moved farther down the corridor.

Seconds later, he lowered her to the floor, and mere moments after that, she stood before him stripped naked, shivering. But not from the cool air circulating in the bedroom. No, from the hooded golden gaze that seemed to gleam bright in the dim room. She forcibly kept her arms by her side, even clenching her fingers into tight fists to fight the impulse to shield herself from his intense scrutiny. A model would be used to baring her body. Still...even though his fingers had been inside her just seconds earlier, heat streamed up her chest, neck, and singed her face. She wasn't a model—she just played one.

"Don't," he said into the tense silence.

"Don't what?" she asked, glancing at the wall of glass that invited Seattle into the room, the sitting area with oversized furniture, the large painting over the huge bed of a marsh with thick trees and foliage at dawn... Anywhere but him.

"You were about to cover yourself. Don't."

Shocked, she jerked her head toward him. "How did you...?"

He didn't answer, instead freed the first three buttons of his shirt and, reaching behind himself, dragged the clothing off in a manner that shouted of his masculinity.

"Watch me," he ordered as his hands dropped to the

waist of his pants.

As if she could do anything else.

With economic movements that were nonetheless sexy for their confidence and lack of pretense, he shoved his pants and boxers to the floor and stood before her in nothing but what he came into this world with and a mural of tattoos covering his arms, shoulders, and chest.

Earlier, she'd seen him clothed in only a pair of football pants, but somehow that one piece of nylon had managed to dampen the power of this man completely nude except for ink. He was...magnificent.

The wide shoulders and chest she'd draped herself over during the photo shoot were the same. But accompanied with the tapered waist and hips, with its helpful and mouthwatering vee that pointed to the nest of dark, tight curls between his powerful thighs, and the thick, long part of him that made him a man, he was art come to life. Under her gaze, his cock thumped against his thigh, sending a shot of two parts excitement, one part feminine anxiety zigzagging through her.

She understood what he was doing; placing them on equal footing. Making himself as vulnerable as she was with his nudity. The gesture calmed her, bolstered her, in a way no amount of pretty or encouraging words could have. That this beautiful giant of a man would do that for her...

Swallowing past the lump of emotion that had no business in this bedroom, she reached for him. And he met her halfway, enfolding her hand in his, and tugging her forward until she pressed against him, shoulder to thigh.

The heat. *God.* The man must have a furnace burning inside of him. Every bit of skin seared her. In the very best of ways.

Desire pumped in her veins, pulsing in her heart, saturating every organ until she *became* desire. Unable to resist touching him one second longer, she traced the dime that hung from a chain and rested in the dip of his collarbone. She still wanted to know the story behind it. But first... She trailed her hand up the outside of his thigh, over his hip, and down between them, closing her fingers around his cock. The heavy, hot weight of him pulsed in her grasp, and she had the inane thought of holding life in her hand. Vulnerable but strong. Fragile, she mused, sliding her other hand lower to cup his balls, but potent.

Letting need guide her, she squeezed his flesh then stroked up, up, up, the ruddy, flared head disappearing in her fist. His entire body went rigid. Except for his hands. They swept up her arms, over her shoulders, and tunneled into her hair. He grunted, pressing his forehead to hers, his hips jerking into her grip. A spasm of pleasure crossed his face when she twisted her wrist and slowly dragged her hand back, greased by the pre-cum pearling on the crown.

She repeated the caress, tugging on his balls, encouraged by the raw sounds of pleasure rumbling from his throat. And with every stroke, every caress, every jerk of his flesh, she grew wetter, hotter, needier. She might've been in control at the moment, but she was quickly losing hers.

"Enough," he barked, closing a fist over hers. "This first time is going to be fast, rough. I can't wait," he admitted with a voice serrated by the same lust that clawed at her.

"I don't care," she breathed, squeezing him again in spite of his restricting hold. "I just want you inside me."

His full mouth firmed into a hard, carnal, almost cruel line. Without warning, he hiked her up into his arms, similar to how he'd positioned her in the living room. But this time, he didn't trap her against a wall. This time, in three long strides, her spine contacted the bed, his body immediately dropping down to cover her.

She wasn't a small woman—not at five-foot-eleven—but

he was much bigger. And with his chest pressing her into the mattress, his shoulders blocking out everything but him, his hips spreading her wide, she felt almost delicate. Protected. Sheltered.

Ensnared.

He shifted, reaching for the bedside table and briefly rummaging in the top drawer before withdrawing a foil packet. In moments, he had the package opened, the condom rolled down his flesh, and the tip nudging her folds. One hand dented the pillow next to her head, and the other clamped the thick root of his cock.

"You ready?" he rumbled, a hard edge to his tone. As if he teetered on the rim of control. *Join the club.*

In response, she spread her thighs wider, skimmed her palms down the sweat-dampened slope of his back, and clutched his muscled ass. With a groan that seemed to start from his taut abdomen and roll up his chest and out of him, he pressed forward. Penetrating her.

She sucked in a breath at the sense of fullness as he parted her, pushing his almost brutish length inside her. Deeper, deeper. Whimpering, she wiggled beneath him, tried to find a position where the...fullness...of his possession didn't threaten to break her in half. The pressure... The discomfort flirted with pain, and she struggled to adjust, just as her sex fluttered and spasmed around his cock in the same attempt.

"Shh," he soothed, pausing, though the stark relief of tendons in his arms as well as the taut delineation of his abdomen telegraphed the cost of his restraint. "It's okay, baby. Let me know when you're ready."

Lust warred with the primitive need to escape this conquering. Forcing herself to relax, she breathed deep, but still clung to him, her purchase in this chaotic, sexual storm. The musky scent of his skin and sex filled her nose. The play of his straining muscles shifted under her fingers. The weight of his huge body pressed her into the mattress. The heavy width of his cock stretched her. But the pain and discomfort ebbed, slowly replaced by a simmering heat that grew with each moment that passed.

"I'm ready," she breathed. Testing that burgeoning heat, she lifted her hips, undulated them. And gasped. Pleasure streaked through her like a bolt of lightning. Surrendering to that seductive lure, she rolled against him again. "Please," she pleaded. "Move."

With a low growl, he slid free of her body, and she dug her heels into the back of his thighs in protest. But with the cockhead lodged just inside her, he thrust forward, lighting up nerve endings she hadn't known existed. She'd granted him permission; he didn't hold back. Both of his hands bracketed her head now, bracing him as he used his whole pagan sex-god body to ride her, work her, drive her to the very edges of insanity. In. Out. In. Out. Grind. He fucked her until all she could do was hang on and take it. Take him. And damn it, did she. He didn't leave one part of her untouched, unclaimed. Unbranded.

Christ, she hadn't known she could go up in flames and still exist. She was Joan of Arc burning at the stake of his erotic hunger, and like that woman, she willingly surrendered, down for the cause.

Her body tightened; a telltale signal of a cataclysm she didn't know she was prepared to face sizzled at the base of spine, in the soles of her feet. She cried out, shaking her head, because she wanted to meet it, combust in it. But at the same time, she feared it, wasn't sure if she would survive the explosion.

But Zephirin didn't give her a choice. Reaching down between them, he pressed his finger to her clit, drawing his thumb around the nub of flesh in a ruthless, demanding circle.

"Give it to me, baby. Let go," he urged, the strain

harshening his voice, tautening his features into a carnal mask of lust. Another rub, another stroke.

And she flew.

Soared.

Then imploded.

Slowly, she opened her eyes, the stars in front of them slowly clearing, the ringing in her ears gradually disappearing. And just in time. As if her orgasm snapped free the leash he'd clipped on his control, Zephirin bucked above her, plunging into her with a power and focus that stole what little breath she'd just recaptured. With one last thrust, he froze. Then his body quaked, shuddered, and a long, low groan wrenched from him.

It was the most erotic thing she'd ever witnessed in her life.

After several moments, he dropped, the support of his arms preventing him from crushing her. But she would've welcomed his weight, loved being covered by him.

He nuzzled her neck, placing an openmouthed kiss along her throat, and Sophia wrapped her arms around his shoulders, a calm—a peace—settling on her after the raging storm of passion.

"Giovanna," he rumbled against her skin.

A shaft of icy cold pierced her chest. Despair, anger, guilt, shame—they roiled inside her, spilling over until that freezing burn turned her into a rigid icicle.

She'd had the most amazing sexual experience of her life and had felt closer to this man than she had to anyone else in years.

And he'd just had sex with her sister.

Chapter Six

"Uhh…are you going to actually lift that or just glare at it for the rest of the afternoon?" Ronin asked from his position behind the weight bench Zephirin lay on. The wide receiver arched an eyebrow, his hands in position under the bar, preparing to spot the 285-pound weight.

Zeph had already put up ten reps, with five more to go. After he finished bench pressing, he'd conclude the workout with bent-over and upright rows. Organized Team Activities, or OTAs, had tied up a couple of hours ago, and only he, Ronin, and Dom remained in the weight room. Good. He didn't feel like putting on an "everything's cool" facade with anyone. Not that anyone with eyes would've believed everything was fine. Not after today's performance during drills and practice.

As if reading his mind, the clang of metal striking metal heralded Dom's appearance next to Ronin. "Something going on you need to get off your chest? I know we all have off days, but you were shit today."

"Yes." With a grunt, Zeph lifted the weight bar, pressed

it to his chest then returned it to the cradle. Exhaling, he slanted Dom a look. "I do want to talk about it. And then afterward, we can braid each other's hair and paint our toenails. Just text me a yes, maybe, or no." He gripped the bar again, did another rep.

"Wow." Ronin smirked. "I thought fucking was supposed to mellow you out. Usually works for me."

Dom snorted. "Maybe that's the problem." He squinted down at Zeph. "Is that the issue? Was Little Zeph only half-cocked, so to speak?"

"Why are you so interested in my dick?" he gritted out between clenched teeth, preparing for another rep. And avoiding both of the boneheads' questions.

Ronin shook his head even as he spotted Zeph, heaving a dramatic sigh. "Your dick today, my balls last night. Maybe we should be talking about what's going on with *you*."

"Shaddup, you." Dom returned his attention to Zeph, the piercing focus and intensity that made him a great quarterback turned full blast on him. "When your pecker is screwing with your head and, by association, the team, then yeah, I'm interested. And even though you're being a complete douche, I'm your friend, too."

"What he said," Ronin added, moving to the free weights and removing them one by one, effectively ending Zeph's workout. Bastard.

But hell, they were right. About his performance today and their entitlement to be concerned. Zeph prided himself on always showing up prepared to work, to show out. Yeah, like Dom said, everyone had a bad day, but too many of them and murmurings started. Questions about if you were losing your edge, the thing that had made you a premier player for your career in the league. And there was always that back-up man ready, waiting, and hungry to snatch your spot.

After his world had gone to hell two years ago, Zeph

couldn't afford to show any weakness. Literally.

Sitting up, he straddled the bench, roughly dragging a hand down his face. Dom leaned against the wall, arms crossed, while Ronin sank onto another bench nearby.

Aside from his grandmother and sister, he was closest to these two men, and yet he didn't know where to start. Not without sounding like a pussy-whipped asshole who hadn't learned his lesson the first time around.

"It's not what you think," he finally said. "I'm not going back there."

He didn't need to go into any more detail than that with his friends, because they knew to what he referred. They'd been there.

Shalene Gallow.

His high school sweetheart, whom he'd broken up with before entering LSU. The woman with whom he'd reconnected with years later, after he'd signed on with the Washington Warriors. At first, he'd believed bumping into her on one of his visits home had been coincidence. But later, after he'd moved her out to Seattle to live with him, he'd discovered how wrong—and naive—he'd been. During their first year in the league, almost all rookies were schooled on what to be aware of, careful of, and flat-out avoid. Women seeking out players so they could reach the so-called status of WAG—Wife and Girlfriend of a sports star—were included in that speech. Knowing this, Zeph had still fallen for the trap...had never suspected the girl-turned-woman whom he'd grown up with, and loved for years, would betray him. For a reality TV show and, in the end, for money.

Shalene had lied and schemed—conspiring with his agent behind his back, renegotiating clauses in his endorsement contracts to benefit her, stealing funds from his accounts. But the biggest lie, the most painful deception, had come after their relationship ended. That lie had almost ripped him in two.

By the time he'd discovered the whole truth, his
season had almost been in the shitter because of his lack of
concentration and focus, new endorsement opportunities
started to dry up, and his team had started to lose their trust
in him.

He refused to return to that place. He was six years into
his football career, when the average one lasted about four
years. And, he was playing at the top of his game. All of his
focus needed to be on football. He refused to allow someone
so inside his head that he risked losing everything he'd worked
and sacrificed for—his grandmother had sacrificed for.

"You sure?" Ronin asked, his tone uncharacteristically
serious.

Zeph stared at him, for a second thinking his friend
questioned whether he would once more place all his trust
in a deceitful woman. Then he replayed the conversation.
Right. Ronin referred to Zeph's assertion that this situation
with Giovanna...or Sophia...differed from Shalene.

"I'm sure," he affirmed. "Hell, for starters, I was head-in-
ass involved with Shalene. Last night was a..." He didn't know
what the hell it was, actually. Well, that wasn't completely
true. He could say it'd been the hottest sex of his life. His
cock had nearly gone into a fucking coma afterward. He
damn sure had. And when he'd awakened, Giovanna/Sophia
had been gone. That still burned. "Last night was one night."

Outside the restaurant, when she'd added that stipulation,
an inexplicable twinge of irritation had vibrated within him,
but he'd squelched it. Relief that he could have her with no
strings, no pretense of commitment had flickered briefly
before even that had been capsized by the lust she'd ignited
in him from the moment she'd walked on the photo set.

"If that's true, then what's with today? And I've seen you
play a game, jump on a plane, grab a couple hours of sleep,

and then get out there and practice. So I don't believe lack of sleep," Dom pried.

Zeph scrubbed a hand over his head. Dom was right, and the knowledge rubbed him raw. One night of sex with her shouldn't have upset his focus. It was the very reason he didn't do relationships. And especially not during football.

"I don't know," Zeph said in response to his friend. He shot to his feet, restless energy surging through him like electric currents. He paced away from them. "It was sex. She left. Stop reading more into it. Is a repeat tempting? Maybe. But the point is, there isn't going to be another night. Football comes first. I'm not risking my career ever again."

"Wait—what? Left?" Ronin cocked his head to the side. "You took her back to your place?"

"Yeah," Zeph replied, tone brusque. He didn't need a secret decoder ring to decipher the astonished expression on both men's faces. Some guys had no problem bringing women back to their homes. Zeph wasn't one of them.

"Again, you sure there isn't something more between you and Giovanna Cruz?" Dom asked, unfolding his arms, his gaze narrowing even more.

"No."

"Do you want there to be?"

Zeph halted mid-pace. Another "no" sprang to his tongue, but he just scowled instead.

"It's been two years, Zeph," Dom continued. "Yeah, me and Ronin might be manwhores, but you've never been. There's no shame in admitting you might want something more than a wham-bam-thank-you-now-get-out-ma'am."

Zeph strode over to where he'd dumped his T-shirt and jerked it on. "I don't want that right now." Maybe not ever. Definitely not with someone whose job required the limelight and fame. Someone who would see him as either a limitless ATM card or a stepping stone in her career. "I just need to get her out of my head."

"Or system," Ronin added, rising to his feet and walking to the corner of the weight room for his own shirt. "Giovanna is a gorgeous woman, no doubt. There's something about her that obviously does it for you. And hell, that's not a bad thing. Go find her, take her back to your place again, and figure it out."

"So basically you're telling me to fuck her out of my system," Zeph drawled.

Ronin splayed a hand over his chest and assumed a wounded air that would've been more convincing if not for the wide grin splitting his grill. "Did I say that?"

Zeph snorted, and Dom shook his head, wearing a smirk.

"I'm going to take a shower. I'll hit you up later. And"— he jerked his chin up—"thanks."

With fist bumps to both men, he headed toward the weight room exit, leaving his friends to argue behind him.

"...not a manwhore, by the way. I think my mother would take exception to that," Ronin complained.

"Well, it's a good thing I didn't call her one, isn't it?" Dom shot back.

Shaking his head, Zeph let the door slam shut behind him. But he couldn't eject Ronin's advice from his head as easily. Everything he'd stated was true—he didn't want a relationship. But he couldn't say the same about not wanting to be back inside Giovanna's body. He hadn't even had a chance to put his mouth on her breasts or discover the undoubtedly sweet taste of her pussy. Due to her disappearing act, he'd been cheated out of having her on her knees in front of him again, only this time with nothing separating her mouth from his cock.

As blunt and even crude as Ronin's suggestion had been, maybe he'd been right.

If she hadn't left him last night, he could've fulfilled at

least half of the images parading through his mind like a porn movie. But since she had snuck out, maybe indulging in some unrestrained, unlimited fucking for a short time would satisfy this insane hunger and allow him to devote all his concentration on where it belonged.

The game.

Since he was a kid, he'd loved football. And to be able to make a living out of his passion was a dream most people would never realize.

A sense of resolve eased through him, and with it a calm. Decision made, he removed his cell from his pocket and quickly dialed a number.

"Wilder Investigations. Jason Wilder speaking," a deep, familiar voice echoed in Zeph's ear.

"Hey, Jason. I need your help. And it's a rush job," Zeph greeted his friend, owner of a private detective firm.

"Shoot."

"I need you to find the home address of someone."

Chapter Seven

"Sophia, can I have a word with you before you go, please?"

Hell no. Go play in traffic. "Sure," she said to her supervisor, Brian Schultz, before turning around to finish shutting down her laptop. And to hide her wince. Not that he would've noticed anyway. He didn't wait for her but pivoted on the heel of his leather Stacy Adams shoes and headed back toward his office.

Most of the time, she loved her job. And then there were the instances she had to deal with Brian "Kneel Before Zod" Schultz. She understood why people committed boss-icide. Sighing, she stowed her computer in her bag and reluctantly followed him down the hall.

"Close the door behind you, please." There wasn't a request in that arrogant tone, and he didn't glance behind him to see if she complied. Instead, he rounded his desk, unbuttoning his suit jacket before lowering to his chair.

Sinking into the armchair flanking his desk, Sophia snuck a peek at her cell phone. It was 5:42 p.m. Damn. She'd been so close to a clean getaway. She should've been out of

FamFit's offices twelve minutes ago. Friday after five o'clock, and her number of fucks given started to rapidly dwindle. Now, sitting in the office of the one person she actively tried to avoid, that total hit zero.

"So," Brian said, leaning back and arching an eyebrow over the rims of his black, hipster glasses. "You were off yesterday."

He fell quiet and studied her, as if his silence would prod her into offering an excuse to explain the reason behind her *scheduled* personal day. Well, he and his faux hawk would be waiting a long-ass time.

Prick.

And not because of his shiny, skinny leg pants, gelled metrosexual hairstyles, and smug, you're-a-peon attitude. Although those were plenty of reasons.

Except when under a tight deadline, for the most part, FamFit boasted a laid-back atmosphere: open floor plan of spacious cubicles with low-walled partitions so people could easily see one another and toss ideas as well as jokes back and forth; a huge break room where at least once a week parties for birthdays, baby showers, or Friday were hosted; and a relaxed dress code where most employees wore jeans, Converse, hoodies, and graphic T-shirts with geek slogans. Case in point, Sophia's current "Back That Thing Up" shirt sporting a thumb drive.

Then there was Brian.

Still, she could deal with his uptightness and personality of a pencil eraser.

No, what made her supervisor a prick and had her aching to go all Grand Theft Auto on his ass was him being a backstabbing thief.

"So," he continued, clearing his throat. "I had a meeting yesterday, and the company is looking to release a new app outside our current weight, exercise, and nutrition trackers.

Something more interactive."

As he continued to speak, excitement and dread twisted inside her belly. Excitement because she loved creating new apps. Everything from the brainstorming of ideas, to the writing code and watching it come to life, to the roll out and waiting on pins and needles to see how the public reacted to it. It was a rush, a heady satisfaction.

Dread because with Brian as a supervisor, any idea had a 99.9% chance of being "stolen" and claimed as his baby. Ethically and professionally, because she worked under him and for FamFit, her work was his and the company's. But morally, promoting her ideas to the Powers that Be as totally his concept and work, without any input from her, was underhanded and low. Especially since he only ever stole from Sophia and the one other female developer in the department. Brian wouldn't dare try that shit with the guys. They might look like extras from *The Big Bang Theory*, but they were positively feral about their work and receiving credit for it. Particularly since credit translated to bonuses and profit-sharing proceeds.

She, on the other hand, was apparently fair game. The first time it'd happened, she'd reluctantly brushed it off, convincing herself that maybe she was being too sensitive. The second time, she'd approached him, and he'd reminded her that she was still new, still had her dues to pay. But that if she continued with the hard work, the next time might be hers. A barrage of words—some of them four-letter and others denigrating his parentage—had weighed down her tongue, but she'd held them back. As a young woman and a minority in a field dominated by white males, she felt like she had to tread carefully. It sucked that she risked being known as the Loud Latina Woman in the office if she dared to stick up for herself.

At twenty-four, she realized how fortunate she was to

work in a career she loved. Yes, she was relatively young, but she'd graduated with dual degrees in computer science and software engineering, and, last year, completed her master's in software development. Not to mention she'd also been building apps since her junior year in college. So, yes, she truly loved her chosen field. But Brian was stealing that joy as surely as he pilfered her ideas and credit. And she had no shame in admitting that she wanted acknowledgment of her hard work. Anyone who claimed differently was a liar or had ambition the size of gnat booty.

Had she called him a prick and thief? She'd meant a misogynistic, backstabbing prick and thief.

"…We have two weeks to deliver a proposal. I've chosen a few of you to submit a concept, and I need it delivered to me in one week. You've proven very innovative in the past, and if yours is chosen, it could mean project manager for you."

Project manager. She'd been at FamFit for three years, and she'd never been appointed to head the numerous teams on which she'd participated. The excitement edged out the unease and resentment. This could be her chance to show not just Brian, but herself, that she could handle the responsibility and succeed. She'd been burned by her supervisor before, but she couldn't turn away from this opportunity for advancement in the company and her field.

"The person whose proposal is accepted will end up project manager?" she asked, needing that verification.

"Yes," Brian replied. "Are you in?"

Sophia smiled, an idea already swirling in her head. "I'm in."

Minutes later, after a quick stop in the bathroom to replace her lip and eyebrow rings, she exited the FamFit office building and stepped into the hustle and bustle of a Friday night in Pioneer Square. Even FamFit's relaxed dress code had a thing about piercings in places other than the ears.

With her keys in hand, she replayed the scene in his office, and her eagerness continued to rise.

This time is going to be different. I just know it. The words ricocheted off the walls of her head, fervent, hopeful, and yeah, with a tinge of desperation.

Her cell phone vibrated in her hand, Cyndi Lauper's "Girls Just Wanna Have Fun" pealing and drawing several amused glances Sophia's way. Without glancing down at the screen, she answered; she'd assigned that ringtone to one person.

"Hey, Vanna," she greeted her sister, entering the parking garage. "Are you on your way home?"

"*Hola, chica!*" Giovanna's cheerful voice echoed clearly across the long-distance connection. After not hearing from her sister for a couple of days, Sophia had missed her. "No, I'm still in Milan."

"What?" Sophia frowned, jabbing the elevator button for the third level. "I thought you wrapped up yesterday and were leaving today. Did you miss your flight?"

Giovanna laughed, and the infectious glee in it had Sophia smiling even though she had no clue why. "You're not going to believe this. I mean, I'm still pinching myself."

"Well, stop that. They'll think the bruises are track marks," Sophia advised.

Her twin snorted. "Only your mind would go there. But, anyway," she continued, and Sophia could easily imagine her swiping a hand through the air as if sweeping aside Sophia's crack-whore observation. "Leo Bianchi himself asked my agent if I could walk in another show he has next Wednesday. Isn't that amazing?" she shrieked.

"Wow, Vanna." Sophia grinned, joy for her sister surging inside her like the accomplishment was her own. "You must've knocked him on his ass. Not that I'm surprised. You're—wait. Does this mean I have to pose as you for something else?"

she asked, suspicion and horror creeping in.

"God, you're paranoid. No," her twin assured her. "I just wanted to let you know I wouldn't be home when planned and to see how the shoot went yesterday. Did I do a fantastic job?"

Reaching her car, Sophia unlocked it and climbed in. "Well, I wasn't outed as an imposter and kicked out, if that's what you're asking," she said, tone wry. "So I guess everything went okay." If by okay, she meant meeting the sexiest man breathing air and having a scorching one-night stand with him, then yep, everything was A-okay.

A pause on the other end. "What aren't you telling me?" Giovanna demanded.

Pinching the bridge of her nose, Sophia leaned her forehead against the steering wheel. Sometimes being the other half of one egg sucked. She sometimes swore that twin ESP crap was a real thing. "Why do you think there's something I'm keeping from you?"

"Oh damn." Giovanna groaned. "Now you're hedging. Some serious shit must've gone down. Spill it. Wait. Just tell me this. Am I going to end up on the cover of a tabloid?"

Sophia blinked. No, she didn't think... Nobody saw her leave with Zephirin last night, right? Well, at least she hadn't noticed any flashing camera phones or photographers...

Another groan sailed down the cell's connection. "Oh God. What did you *do*?"

"First off, I think you're tabloid-cover-free," Sophia assured her twin.

"You think," Giovanna gritted out. "I'm dead."

"Look," Sophia said on the end of a sigh. Not like she could keep this from her twin. Not when, technically, it'd been Giovanna having the one-night stand. Even if in name only. "You didn't tell me I would be modeling with Zephirin Black."

"Did it matter?" Giovanna countered. "You don't know a football from a whiffle ball. I definitely didn't think you'd recognize him."

"Okay, you got a point there. But still, you should've prepared me for *him*. I mean, the man is gorgeous. A hazel-eyed Shemar Moore with a shaved head. A little heads up would've been nice. Something like, 'Now, Sophia, be prepared to meet Zeph Black. He's sex walking, so make sure you wear both flame-retardant and water-resistant underwear.' But nope, you let me walk into that one like a lamb to slaughter. So in essence, this is fifty percent your fault—"

"*Madre de Dios!*" Giovanna gasped. "You had sex with him."

Hah. Sex. That hadn't been sex; she'd had sex before. That was…the fucking unicorn. Fabled. Heard of. But never seen and damn sure never experienced. Wincing, Sophia shook her head back and forth on the wheel. "Yes and no."

"What the hell does that mean? That's like being a little pregnant. Either you fucked him or you didn't," she yelled.

"I mean, I did. But he may have, y'know, thought it was you." Bracing herself for the imminent explosion, she curled the fingers of her free hand around the steering wheel.

"This is *Twin of Fire*. Holy hell, I'm living a romance novel," came the whispered reply.

Not the response Sophia had been expecting. Blinking, she lifted her head. "Huh?"

"*Twin of Fire* by Jude Devereaux. Remember? The one twin was engaged, and she asked her sister to pretend to be her and take her place on a date for just one night. The sister ended up going to bed with the fiancé, and all the time, he believed he was with the other twin, his betrothed."

"Betrothed?" Sophia snickered. Couldn't help it.

"Shut up, you. Anyway, the whole charade exploded

in both of the twins' faces. So how well do you think this is going to end?" Giovanna snapped.

"I know, I know," Sophia muttered. "Not about the book, because I don't know what the hell you're talking about with that. But Zephirin? It's a mess. He thought he was with you. Even called me by your name."

"Okay, one. Eew. And two, I'm sorry, Fi." Her voice softened. "That had to hurt. If *you* slept with him after knowing him for a matter of hours, you must've really been into him."

And the upside to having someone able to read her mind was Sophia didn't have to explain her feelings. Giovanna just *knew*.

"Yeah, it did hurt," she murmured. "Even though it's stupid, right? I went in with my eyes open."

"Irrational, yes. But not stupid."

A beat of silence passed between them. Then Giovanna's laughter reverberated in Sophia's ear, and her own filled the car.

"You do realize you have to let it go, don't you?" Giovanna counseled. "You didn't lie to him on purpose, but just thinking back on the brooding, uh, hard, man from the one time we worked together, I can't see him accepting that as an excuse."

"No, you're right." Staring out the windshield, she conjured up an image of an intense, broody Zephirin. Not that she had to try too hard. Since she'd met him, that picture had hovered at the edge of her consciousness, refusing to be banished. "I told him it was just that one night. I can't go on lying to him. And telling him the truth would risk your reputation and career. So, yeah, I don't intend to continue anything beyond last night." Sophia shook her head. "I hate that I put you in this position, though. Seeing him from now on is going to be incredibly awkward for you."

"Nothing I can't handle," Giovanna assured her. "Don't worry about it. Just...take care of yourself, okay? On one hand, I'm actually glad you did something impulsive. Sometimes you act like an old maid on the verge of a trip to the pet store for the first of fifty cats. But still. I don't want you hurt. Especially when you were doing me a favor."

"I'm fine." Sophia waved off her twin's concern even though she couldn't see the gesture. "And a cat is a companion, not an indictment on a person's social relationships."

"Uh-huh," Giovanna drawled. "It's one o'clock in the morning here, so I need to get some sleep. But can you go by my place, check on it, water the plants, and grab my mail?"

"Sure thing," Sophia agreed, turning the key in the ignition. "Be safe, okay? And don't forget to call Mom and let her know about your extended stay before she blows my phone up."

Who was she kidding? Their mother would phone Sophia anyway, complaining about all the dangers and pitfalls a young, single girl could encounter in a foreign country. Sophia rolled her eyes but smiled. Alicia Cruz was the epitome of a worry wart.

"I will. One more thing though... Since you did use my name, I think it's only fair that I know if he's as...big...as the rest of him. Like, are you walking funny today?"

"Bye, Giovanna."

Grinning, Sophia hung up on her sister's cackling.

But as she drove out of the parking deck into the summer evening traffic, that smile dimmed. Her twin was correct; Sophia had done the right thing by limiting sex with Zephirin to one night. Anything—a relationship, a friendship, friends with benefits—based on lies was doomed to failure. And maybe she could find Zephirin and confess the truth to him. But the reason she hadn't yesterday still remained. She wouldn't jeopardize her sister's career.

And then there stood the reason she couldn't admit to her twin...could barely confess to herself.

What if Zeph preferred her sister over the real Sophia?

It was a possibility. When compared to glamorous, outgoing, gorgeous, sophisticated Giovanna, Sophia—shyer, fashion-challenged, hermit, sometimes rude, at times awkward—couldn't compete. High school had taught her that, as well as the few men she'd dated who had either courted her just to get close to Giovanna or, worse, had forgotten about Sophia as soon as they laid eyes on her more dazzling half and had fallen for her twin.

It smacked of cowardice, but after witnessing that admiring, lustful gleam enter one too many men's eyes after spotting Giovanna, Sophia wasn't willing to risk that happening with Zephirin.

Nope, better to cut things off with him before he could disappoint her.

Before he shattered her.

Chapter Eight

Zephirin frowned as he stopped before the door of the address Jason had texted to him an hour earlier. Zeph remembered Giovanna telling him she lived in Alaska Junction, but Jason had sent him to this apartment in an older but well-kept, pretty building in the heart of Belltown, about ten minutes from the photography studio. How could he forget? The reason he'd chosen his place over hers last night had been the location; his downtown condo had been closer than the twenty minutes to her Alaska Junction home.

He lifted his fist to knock on the door, the question still rolling around in his head. But before his hand could connect, the door opened, revealing the object of his inexplicable fascination. She gaped at him, eyes wide, lips parted in an "O" of surprise.

Slowly, he lowered his arm. Even knowing he stared at her like some kind of starstruck teenager, he still couldn't remove his gaze from her. Not when he'd spent the entire day rewinding and replaying the night before. The sweet, addictive taste of those full, sensual lips. The glow of her bare skin.

The wet, hot embrace of her sex. The haze of pleasure taking over those pretty eyes as she came so hard, so uninhibited. His cock throbbed, hardening as the images scrolled across his mind like a peep show. With the force of a will he hadn't known he possessed, he kept his hands down at his sides instead of reaching out and dragging her against him. That mouth with its pierced bottom lip. It was a temptation that would've sent Adam into sin quicker than that apple.

Today, in a T-shirt, skinny jeans, and flip-flops, her blue-tipped hair in one of those topknots, she appeared less like an up-and-coming supermodel and more like one of the everyday women sipping lattes in one of Seattle's coffee shops. Or one of the internet cafes.

"Nice shirt."

She glanced down at the thumb drive graphic under the words "Back That Thing Up," a frown furrowing her forehead, then returned her attention to him. "What are you doing here?" she demanded, still wearing the scowl.

Ignoring that question since he had yet to fully answer it for himself, he instead nodded toward her apartment. "Can I come in?"

Her teeth sank into the lush curve of her bottom lip, and for a moment, he thought she was going to deny him. But then she gave her head a small shake and stepped back, allowing him entrance. Taking immediate advantage before she could change her mind, he strode past her.

He studied the spacious studio apartment, taking in the wide windows that added an illusion of more space, the exposed brick walls, hardwood floors, and eclectic array of furniture. He assumed the floor-to-ceiling Japanese screen hid the bed from the rest of the room, separating the area into the living section and the bedroom. Pretty and stylish, it somehow still didn't jibe with the woman in front of him. He couldn't put his finger on it, but something seemed to be missing. As soon as the thought passed through his head, he dismissed it with a scoff. One night of sex didn't mean he knew her.

"I thought you lived in Alaska Junction," he said, voicing the question that still nagged at him.

The door closed behind him, and she crossed the small distance separating them, arms crossed. His gaze dipped to her breasts; no force on earth could've kept him from looking. Not after he now knew in vivid, intimate detail how the dark brown tips contrasted with her coffee and cream skin. Or the slight weight of them in his hand.

"Hey. Excuse me. Up here," she snapped, pointing toward her face. "I definitely don't live in my tits."

The polite, gentlemanly thing to do would be to apologize.

"Sorry," he said.

"Hashtag not sorry," she muttered.

He controlled the quirk of his lips before they could betray his amusement. She was right. He wasn't sorry. She had a body that deserved to be worshipped. From the firm thrust of flesh under her funny-as-hell T-shirt to the feminine flare of hips and long display of slender, toned legs shown to perfection in the tight jeans—she had him a breath away from falling on his knees and burying his face between those beautiful thighs. Thighs he knew would spread for him in abandoned welcome like they had the night before.

Slowly, he retraced his visual path back up her tall frame, finally meeting her eyes, the piercing in her eyebrow glinting under the lighting. Those chocolate eyes that couldn't hide the arousal darkening them. He'd bet his left nut that under those crossed arms, her nipples stood at strict attention.

"Alaska Junction?" he asked again, his voice as rough as churned-up gravel.

Her shoulders stiffened, and she turned away from him, heading toward the small kitchen nook. Like she was a magnet, he followed, leaning a shoulder against the adjoining wall.

"Do you want something to drink?" She pulled open the refrigerator door. "I have water, juice, or wine."

"I'm fine," he said, waiting for an answer.

Withdrawing a bottle of water, she closed the door and faced him. "I've only been here a short time. I guess 'home' is still my old apartment until I get used to living here."

He nodded; it made sense. He'd lived in the downtown condo for a couple of years now, but the house in Redmond had been his home for the four years he and Shalene had been together. Sometimes the apartment still felt like a place he crashed after games, not a home with memories. But that wasn't necessarily a bad thing, either.

"This is a nice place," he said.

And just managed not to punch himself in the face. He'd never been one for small talk—it'd always seemed a complete waste of words and time. Not to mention painful, like right now. Hell, he'd been deep inside her body, talking shouldn't be this damn difficult. He scanned the area, and seconds later, his scrutiny landed on the tall curio cabinet that housed a surprisingly huge collection of DVDs instead of knickknacks. Not requesting her permission, he pushed off the wall and moved across the floor to the cabinet.

Horror movies. Comedies. Action. Fantasy. But three shelves were devoted to movies of the eighties and early nineties. *St. Elmo's Fire*, of course. *Pretty in Pink. The Breakfast Club. Some Kind of Wonderful. Back to the Future.* Parts one, two, *and* three.

"I notice a theme going on here," he observed. "But *Back to the Future Three*? I wasn't even aware anyone had actually seen that one."

"The whole series is a classic," she sniffed, her arms slowly unfolding as some of the defensiveness in her posture peeled away. "All of them are. They were the gold standard of original movie making. *Lost Boys*. First teenage vampire movie. *Dirty Dancing*. Became a phenomenon between the movie, the music, and Patrick Swayze's hips. God, I still miss him." She sighed, then continued. "*Mystic Pizza*. Launched the careers of Julia Roberts and Vincent D'Onofrio. Before there was Bobby Goren and Wilson Fisk, there was Bill Montijo. And let's not even get started on how *Say Anything* gave us John Cusack."

"Uh-huh." He cocked his head to the side, studying her animated expression. "You're a romantic."

She stared at him. Snorted. "Boy, did you miss the boat on that one."

"Did I?" He shifted closer, closing the distance between them in slow increments like a trainer approaching a spooked mare. She reminded him of that elegant, wary animal. He had the sense if he rushed her, she would run as far from him as this studio apartment would allow. That both worried and intrigued him. "All of those movies have one thing in common. They're romances or have romance in them. Is that why you watch them, Giovanna? Is that what you want? Someone to see you, date you, take care of you?"

"I can take care of myself," she said, her voice a decimal above a whisper. "And I asked you to call me Sophia."

That's right. Giovanna was the model, the persona. Sophia was the tatted, pierced, guarded but passionate woman beneath. If he were smart, he would insist on calling her Giovanna. Keep the fact that she was a model whose visibility could only be boosted by dating a pro football player front and center in his mind.

Yeah, if he were smart…

"I know you can, Sophia," he deliberately added the name. Screw it. Calling her Sophia was a small concession. Besides, Sophia somehow seemed to fit this version of her more. "But sometimes don't you want someone else to handle the load? Ease the pressure of the day, touch you, make you forget?"

Soft puffs of breath echoed in the room like the report of gunshots. Her chest rose and fell, wide eyes fixed on him. The term "deer in headlights" came to mind.

"I'm not having sex with you again," she stated, panic—if he wasn't mistaken—edging her voice. Though he couldn't help but notice that her gaze skimmed down his body, the arousal darkening her eyes unmistakable.

"Who said anything about sex?" he asked, even as his mind and dick seemed to throb in protest. "Where's your mind at, Sophia?"

The alarm evaporated from her expression, replaced by a scowl. "What are you doing here? I thought we agreed to one night." Her frown deepened. "And do I even want to know how you found this address?"

He shrugged. "Probably not. And we agreed to one night of sex. I'm not here for that. I want to invite you to dinner."

"Dinner?" she repeated, skepticism soaking her tone like a wet, heavy blanket.

Her suspicion didn't disappear. Smart woman. Because he—who despised lying—was doing it through his teeth. All he could think about was having her under him again. Then, after a breather, over him. Then in front of him. Hunger clawed at his gut like a caged beast demanding to be fed.

"Yes. Have you eaten?" Not exactly the kind of craving he wanted to satisfy, but maybe she would lower her guard if he played nice.

He saw the indecision playing out on her expressive face. Also noted the moment she decided to tell the truth. "No," she grudgingly admitted. She shook her head. "This is a bad idea. Just...bad," she said in a low voice.

"Why?" He moved even closer, this time surrendering to

the need to just touch. Pinching her chin between his thumb and forefinger, he tilted her head back as he shifted into her personal space. Eliminating it. "What are you afraid of, baby?"

"That," she whispered. Her lids lowered, hiding her eyes from him, and he almost demanded she open them. "Zephirin, I…" She exhaled a shaky breath and stepped back, dislodging his hand from her face. Tunneling her fingers through her hair, she nearly toppled the bun on top of her head, but she didn't seem to notice. Pivoting, she crossed the living area and halted in front of an arched window. "I'm so not who you think I am," she murmured, voice so low he barely caught her words.

"Then let me find out," he said, staring at the rigid line of her spine. "Introduce me to Sophia. Introduce her to me."

"And if you don't like her?"

"I will, if you give me the chance. Trust me with her, and I won't reject her."

A sense of urgency vibrated under his skin like a forewarning that if he didn't convince her now, he would lose the opportunity to discover all the hidden passion in this woman. Unable to remain where he stood, he traced her steps and didn't stop until his palms flattened against the wall above her head, and his chest was pressed to her back. She stiffened but didn't move away. He lowered his head, his mouth hovering next to her ear. Her flower and fruit scent, the same that had been more condensed, muskier with her arousal the night before, enveloped him in a warm, sexy embrace. The two dark brown beauty marks behind the curve of her ear taunted him, begged for his tongue.

He swallowed the growl that rolled up his chest and into his throat. "Dinner. That's it."

She turned, facing him. He could easily read the indecision in the gaze that met his. "That's it?"

"Yes," he said. The urge to touch her surged within him, brutal and demanding. He surrendered to the need and brushed the full curve of her bottom lip with his thumb. But that was all he allowed himself. He shifted back a small step. "Sophia, you're focused on your career, and so am I. Everything else takes a back seat to it. I've let relationships..." *Fuck me up.* "...distract me before, and I'm not willing to risk my career like that again. I can't offer anyone a long-term commitment. I want to be as upfront with you as you were with me last night."

She studied him for several long, quiet seconds. "And you don't want to risk getting into a relationship with someone who could lie to you...again."

He didn't reply to her amazingly accurate assumption. But from the understanding that seemed to shadow her eyes, he didn't need to.

Another moment passed. Then another. But finally... "Okay. Dinner."

He breathed.

Chapter Nine

She was going to hell.

Sophia sat at the marble bar in Zephirin's state-of-the-art kitchen, watching him prepare their meal with an efficiency that struck her as endearing and a little intimidating.

And hot. Good Lord, definitely hot.

As someone whose diet consisted of anything not cooked by her, she appreciated the coordination and weird kind of beauty that went into it as he prepared several dishes at once. Shifting from the stove to the huge island in the middle of the room and back. Chopping vegetables and sautéing them. Baking fish. He was poetry in motion, and though she'd never seen him play, she could easily imagine him showing the same grace and economy of movement on the field. For such a huge man, he moved with a fluidity that was both poetic, elegant, and powerful.

Or maybe it was just Zephirin.

Aaaand her ogling reminded her of exactly why her soul was sentenced to eternal damnation.

This lust and fascination for this beautiful, sin-wrapped-in-flesh man.

Back at Giovanna's apartment, she should've said no to his invitation. Put her foot down. Remembered that not an hour earlier, she'd promised her sister she would end whatever the…thing was between her and Zephirin. The fact that she'd had to lie to him about the apartment should've been a clear and blaring reminder of why even entertaining seeing him again fell under the heading of Worst Fucking Idea Ever.

"I've been lied to so often, the truth is my white whale."

For a moment, when he'd asked her to trust him, promised that he wouldn't reject her, she'd almost confessed everything. The favor for her twin to take her place on the photo shoot. Her decision to take one night for herself with him and not see him again. Why she'd snuck out of his bed after hearing him whisper her sister's name. Everything.

But then she'd remembered those bleak, hard words he'd stated in the bar. This was a man accustomed to being lied to, to having his choices stolen from him. And he would see her as one more thief. And coward that she was, she hadn't wanted to see his disappointment…his disgust.

Hell, if she had one ounce of the sense that people believed she possessed in spades, she would've rejected his offer for dinner. Cauterized the harm.

But knowing and doing were two different things. She should've said no and shown him the door—her sister's door. But after he'd asked her to introduce him to Sophia, the cracks and fissures fractured her already flimsy barricade of resistance. More than anything, she wanted him to meet her—the *real* her. But right on the heels of that longing came the voice reminding her that Zeph wouldn't like the "real her." In that Google search, she'd also seen the women he'd been pictured with. Gorgeous, stylish, poised, and confident. Women like Giovanna, not her.

And yet, here she sat. Watching him. Lusting after him

with the words "no sex" reverberating in her head like a mantra. Even as her wet panties mocked her.

Hell. She smothered a snort. Forget going to hell. She was in it.

Yet the realization didn't stop her from staring at the fit of the jeans over his trim hips, thick thighs, and ass. She suppressed a groan. *That ass.* Her fingers had clutched the firm flesh last night, and she swore she could still feel the hardness of it against her skin now. Swiftly, she dragged her gaze up to the T-shirt that hugged the muscles of his shoulders, upper arms, and wide chest. Ink painted his lower arms. The V-neck offered her a peek at the powerful column of his throat and collarbone, also baring the slim necklace with its pierced dime that nestled in the shallow dip at the bottom of his throat. If someone had told her she would be jealous of a coin, she would've offered them a Xanax and a glass of wine.

"Can I ask you a question?" She propped her elbows up on the bar top. He glanced up at her from stirring vegetables and nodded. "What does the dime mean? Is it something special?"

"My grandmother gave it to me before I left for college. It's an old Creole superstition. Wearing a pierced dime around your neck is supposed to ward off the devil."

Sophia blinked. "Um...wow."

He huffed out a low laugh. "When I pointed out that as a Catholic, she shouldn't believe superstition, she told me this had nothing to do with God and everything to do with the devil, so just shut up and wear the damn thing. And that's a direct quote."

The humor and obvious love in the deep timbre of his voice had her chest squeezing even as she loosed a bark of laughter. "She sounds amazing. Feisty."

"She is," he murmured. "She's my rock." Switching the

flame off underneath the food, he arched an eyebrow. "Tell me something about you."

Right. She was supposed to be introducing herself to him. The real her. The her that he could truly never know because she'd been lying to him about herself since the beginning. The her that would probably bore him in three-point-two seconds flat.

Shoving the thought—and the guilty twist inside her—aside with the power of a backhoe, she shrugged. "I speak several languages." She'd grown up in a Spanish-speaking household as her parents were both Puerto Rican. Still, since she was younger, she'd always had an affinity for different tongues. They fascinated her, challenged her. And when she'd been a kid, she'd had dreams of traveling to foreign countries, visiting all the cities that had always fascinated her. London. Paris. Madrid. Manila... Middle Earth. "Five including English...and if you count Elvish."

He stared at her. Blinked. "Excuse me? Elvish? As in pointy-eared, long-haired, bow and arrow elves?"

Again, she shrugged, suddenly wishing she'd kept her mouth shut instead of opening it and proving what a geek she was. Hell, half the people she worked with were fluent in Klingon.

"Don't get shy now." A corner of his mouth quirked as he turned fully toward her and planted his palms on the bar. "Say something. Please."

"*Lle naa vanima edan.*" *You are a beautiful man.* A sentiment she was too embarrassed to confess in English.

Slowly, a full-fledged, heart-stopping, gorgeous grin spread across his face. *Goddamn.* No wonder the man didn't do that often. He had to use his smile like the nuclear codes. Carefully, rarely, and only in important circumstances. Otherwise, this world would be rendered to ash from all the exploding ovaries.

"Damn, that's sexy as hell," he said, shaking his head, still wearing that coronary-inducing grin. "What did you say?"

As if she'd reveal that. "Learn it if you want to find out." She issued the challenge with a tilt of her head.

"Maybe I will," he replied, and the soft tone conjured an image of him snatching up a thrown down gauntlet. Although the idea of him actually learning the language of—how had he put it?—"the pointy-eared, long-haired, bow and arrow" race of Tolkien fell somewhere between ludicrous and *really* ludicrous.

"What are the others?" he asked.

"*Yo quisiera lamberte su cuerpo entero.*" Spanish. *I would really love to just lick you all over right now.* "*Mais c'est fou de te vouloir.*" French. *But wanting you is crazy.* "*Pero hindi ko matulungan sarili ko.*" Tagalog or Filipino. *But...I can't help myself.*

He studied her, and while she wanted to duck her head and avoid his scalpel-sharp scrutiny, she met it. Only because he couldn't know the revealing words she'd uttered in the different languages.

"Why is it crazy to want me?" Her face must've betrayed the shock blasting through her, because he added, "I'm Creole. I know some French."

She glanced everywhere—anywhere—but at him. How could she tell him the truth? That wanting him was crazy because he believed her to be someone else. And the more time she spent with him, the longer she let him think she was her twin, the deeper in lies she sank...and dragged him with her.

But no way in hell could she admit that. She cleared her throat, stalling for time. Praying a credible answer would materialize. "I—"

The timer on the oven dinged, announcing the fish he'd placed inside twenty minutes earlier was done. *Oh thank*

God. Saved by the bell. Literally.

He transferred his attention to the food, removing the dish and setting it on top of the stove. But seconds later he returned with a chunk of pink, flaky meat pinched between his fingers.

"Open," he ordered.

She complied without hesitation, and he slid the piece of salmon between her parted lips, setting it on her tongue. He didn't remove his finger...made her lick the underside of it as she swallowed the food. And he still didn't withdraw. In that instant, she had a choice. Remind him—and herself—of her "no sex" rule. Or indulge in this small, not-so-innocent flirtation. She didn't have to let it go any further.

Okay, so she'd started not only lying to Zephirin, but to herself, too.

Still didn't stop her from curling her tongue around his finger. From sucking on it. Drawing it deeper. Stroking it. Grazing it with her teeth.

Didn't stop her from closing her eyes and enjoying the hard, calloused texture of skin. From substituting his finger for his cock in her imagination. Except even her dreams didn't stretch that far. Her biblical knowledge of him couldn't forget how much thicker, heavier, wider his flesh was.

Her breath like a buzz saw in her lungs and head, she pulled back...but not before treating herself to one last lick. She lifted her lashes and almost toppled off the bar stool. The explosive heat in those golden eyes was a punch of lust straight to her chest. His mouth formed a hard but sensual line, his jaw clenched tight. She'd seen lust on him last night, but under the glaring lights of the kitchen, the emotion appeared harsher. Hungrier.

She clutched the edge of the counter as if holding on for dear life. Didn't let go even as he rounded the bar. Even as he crowded her against the marble, his chest pressing against her spine as it had earlier at her sister's apartment. His arms bracketing hers, his large hands settling on either side of hers. She felt...covered. If they were in bed, she would've been mounted. The image sizzled along her synapses, causing them to misfire. She blamed the phenomenon on her inability to move out of the cage of his arms and body.

"Do it again." The low, rumble of his voice vibrated against her back, over her skin. She shivered as he rubbed the tips of two fingers over her bottom lip. "Let me in."

Unable to deny him, or herself if she were brutally honest, she opened her mouth. Permitted him to penetrate, to fill her. His groan rolled through her, sliding under her shirt and stroking her skin. Knowing that his eagle gaze watched his fingers disappear inside her was a caress to the aching, pulsing flesh between her thighs. She squeezed her legs together, but all the gesture did was remind her how empty she was. How desperate she was to have him bury his cock in her sex as slowly and deliberately as his fingers did her mouth.

As she'd done moments ago, she sucked him, savoring the hint of spices from the food he'd prepared. Moaning at the darker, more unique flavor of *him*. She raked him with the edge of her teeth, lapped at the slight abrasion. With a low growl, he withdrew his hand until his fingertips rested on her lip...then pushed back inside, demanding more of her touch.

"Damn, that's so pretty." His gritty praise sent pleasure stumbling through her. "So goddamn pretty." He repeated the strokes, imitating the erotic possession of his body over hers from the previous evening.

At some point, she'd released her hold on the counter and grasped his thick wrists, her nails digging into his skin.

"I thought about this all day, Sophia. Had a shitty practice because I couldn't focus." He didn't cease taking her mouth. His thrusts between her lips shortened, hardened. And she loved it, sucked harder. "Not with images of you taking my dick just like you are now in my head. Beautiful. Sweet. And hot as hell."

Jesus, he had to stop talking or any moment, she would go up in flames. Her sex clenched, quivering in readiness for a deep, rough ride. One more night of sex. Just one. Then tomorrow, she would walk away. Like she should've tonight if she weren't so damn weak.

She shifted, tried to turn around in his arms, but he prevented the movement with his body. One hand burrowed through her hair, tangling, gripping. He tugged her head back and withdrew his fingers from her mouth. Slowly, he trailed the damp tips down her chin and neck, coming to rest in the point of her shirt's V neckline. He paused, and she was acutely aware that with a shift of only centimeters to the left or the right, he could be teasing her nipples into tighter points.

She bit her lip, unable to think of another surefire way of trapping the plea inside her.

"I want to renegotiate," he murmured in her ear. "One night wasn't enough for me. I didn't get a chance to discover everything about this gorgeous body. Didn't get the opportunity to find out what makes you shiver, scream... come. So here are the terms." He brushed his lips over her jaw, giving her just a hint of tongue. "We fuck until we get our fill. You don't want strings? Fine, neither do I. You want to walk away whenever you're done? Me, too. But until then, you let me have you. And you can have me in return."

If the devil hadn't uttered something similar to Eve when tempting her with that apple, then he'd been phoning it in. Because if he'd come at her with the sinful, dirty lure Zephirin had just thrown at her, Eve wouldn't have stopped at one apple. She would've gorged on that whole damn tree.

She squeezed her eyes shut, but the absence of vision only intensified the tingling in her scalp from his fingers in her hair and the texture of his full lips on her skin. Made her more aware of his touch between her breasts.

Say no. Say no. Say no.

The chant reverberated and pinged off her skull like a ricocheting bullet, gaining speed with each pass. *Saynosaynosayno.*

But before she could utter a denial—or acceptance—he released her. For a moment, the abrupt absence of his touch left her reeling. Like being shoved face first into a snow bank after the toasty warmth of a heat-filled car. Inhaling deeply, she didn't loosen her grip on the counter, tracking him as he returned to his position on the other side of the bar.

"I just have one condition, one rule," he said, the sexy growl gone from his voice. Sliding his hands in the front pockets of his pants, he faced her, his face inscrutable.

She appreciated rules, had lived her life by them. Her work required them in the form of codes. And with him, she definitely needed some kind of boundaries. "Okay," she breathed. "I'm listening."

He studied her for a long, weighty moment, his eyes capturing hers. Refusing to free her.

"Playing ball is all I've ever wanted to do, and I love the game. But with it comes the baggage. You learn everyone doesn't have your best interest at heart. That people will try and get close to you simply for what you can do for them or what they can get out of you. It's an environment that breeds greed and mistrust. That's why last night, when you added the stipulation of only one night, your honesty took me by surprise, and I admired it. I was grateful for it because it's so rare."

He leaned back against the marble island, and his gaze seemed to turn inward as if staring at something only he could see.

"I'm going to be just as truthful with you, Sophia. As upfront as I can. I was in a relationship that imploded because of dishonesty. Her lies almost stole my career. Almost des—" He broke off abruptly, his jaw clenching. After a moment, he continued, but that flat note had entered his voice again. The same one from the previous night when their conversation had turned to lies. "That's my one rule, Sophia. Honesty, no lies. Ever."

The words "no lies" assaulted her conscience like a battering ram. Dread and a deep, heavy sadness weighed on her chest like a massive boulder. She'd already broken that rule.

"Another thing. I can't offer you anything more than this." He waved a hand back and forth between them. "I'm telling you this because I don't want to mislead you. I can give you more of last night. But that's all. Anything else—a relationship, a commitment—I don't have to give. Will I ever? Maybe after football. If I do, though, it will be with someone completely outside of this business."

"So, it's not that you can't offer a relationship. You just can't extend it to me." Or Giovanna. Christ, this was confusing. So was the inexplicable stab of hurt and anger.

His expression solemn, he nodded. "I've already done that. I've seen the wreckage fame and celebrity, or the desire for them, can inflict. Jealousy. Competition. Mistrust. Resentment. Home should be a sanctuary, not a combat zone."

The irony that her true job would fulfill his "perfect mate" requirement wasn't lost on her. The real Sophia wasn't in "the business." At twenty-eight years old, he could still have several good years of playing football ahead of him, and he seemed determined to spend those years alone.

"Is that it?" She moved her hands to her lap and out of his sight, so he couldn't glimpse the tight, knuckle-whitening clasp of her fingers. "No-strings sex and no lies. Do I have it all covered?"

"No." Slowly, he straightened and crossed the space separating them. Flattening his palms on the bar counter, he leaned forward until their faces were centimeters apart. Until she could taste his kiss on his breath. "I want you. I want to suck on that full, sexy-ass bottom lip, taste you, touch you. It's taking everything in me not to pull you on this counter, pull down those jeans, and bury myself inside you until you come, screaming my name." His gaze dropped to her mouth, remained there for several seconds before sliding up again. "Now I'm finished."

Oh God. She released a shuddering breath, knowing he heard it. Felt it on his lips. This man was temptation in flesh.

If she had any integrity, any sense of self-preservation, she would step away now. Nothing could come of this... arrangement. She should rise from this stool, thank him for the dinner invite, and walk out the door.

But she didn't. Because the truth was, she couldn't. When was the last time she'd wanted something, *anything*, as desperately as she craved him? Never. Nothing had ever carved out this hollow cavity that could only be filled by the pleasure he'd introduced her to the night before. Nothing had ever made her feel so...feminine. Beautiful. Needed.

God, that admission made her sound so pathetic. And she didn't care. She'd never stepped out on a limb and went after something she wanted, grabbed it for her own. Even FamFit had pursued her. She'd always been too scared of disappointment. Her past with the bullying, with men, with the often unfair comparisons between her and Giovanna had left her paralyzed, willing to settle instead of facing possible rejection.

But here, in this high-end kitchen, Zephirin offered her a chance to have him. Have her moment in time. Hell, he'd even handed her an out, a reason to call it quits. She—the model "she"—wasn't what he desired in a partner anyway.

And in the end, they would walk away, leaving behind only memories.

Could she live with that, even knowing he believed her to be someone else?

Yes, her body screamed. But her mind hesitated, inserting a red flag of caution she had no choice but to heed.

She could accept his terms, but at what cost? To him? To her?

Because one thing she knew for certain. He might be used to no-strings-attached relationships, but she wasn't. If anyone had asked her before this moment, she would've claimed she wasn't built for sex-only, emotionally barren attachments. She still believed it. And yet, she stood on the cusp of diving headfirst into one. With Zephirin Black. A man she had the sneaking suspicion possessed the power to hurt her beyond anyone else.

God.

She had to tell him.

She slid off the stool. Shuddering out a breath, she lifted her gaze to his hooded one. The lust hadn't abated, but a watchfulness had entered his scrutiny.

"Zephirin," she began. Stopped. Inhaled, and tried again. "There's something I need to te—"

"No."

She blinked at the abrupt interruption. "Sorry?"

"Sophia, I want you," he said in that same blunt manner. The no-nonsense, unequivocal statement sent a flash of heat barreling through her. "I might not want a relationship, but since I woke up this morning with the scent of sex on my sheets, all I can think about is being inside you again. And again. Until I satisfy this craving, or you get enough. Either or, I don't care, just as long as I'm inside you."

He rounded the counter, and his big body crowded into her space, stealing her breath.

"Let me make myself crystal clear. I don't need feelings—I don't want them. This...arrangement between us can be so good and easy for both of us. So please don't muddy it up with anything deeper than sex and orgasms. We can have each other and just enjoy it. So if whatever you plan on telling me will make this deeper than it needs to be and prevent me from taking you, then let it go."

The moisture in her mouth had evaporated the moment he uttered "scent of sex on my sheets" in that low, sensual molasses drawl. His invitation to let it go and enjoy the temporary, hot-sex-on-a-platter time they could have together tempted her like chocolate-dipped coffee beans. He didn't want her confession, and if this...thing he offered was only meant to be short term before they went their separate ways, what harm could it do to give in? To surrender and take this brief interval in the everyday-ness of her life for herself?

She just didn't *know*. Right and wrong had seemed so easy to decipher before the offer of brain-melting sex had been thrown in the mix.

"I...I need time to think it over," she said. "I think I'm going to skip dinner. Thank you, though."

He nodded, and while he didn't appear angry, she couldn't miss the tension riding his body. "I'll take you home."

Those four words should've sent relief spiraling through her. Instead, she had to force herself not to ask him to let her stay.

Forget going to hell.

She was going crazy.

Chapter Ten

She hadn't said no.

But five days had passed since Friday night when Zeph had reopened negotiations with Sophia, and she damn sure hadn't said yes either.

Actually, she hadn't said much of anything, even though before she'd exited his car he'd entered his contact information into her phone. To be fair, other than a text last night inviting her to today's camp, he hadn't reached out to her either. He wanted to give her space to make a decision. But damn, granting her time and distance was leaving him with a torturous case of blue balls.

The piercing blow of a whistle snatched him out of his thoughts, and he focused on the present. The present being day two of the football summer camp he sponsored through his Jaybird Foundation, named after his grandmother's nickname. He'd founded the nonprofit organization five years ago to provide support and assistance to inner-city and underprivileged kids across the nation through football. His vision had been to help the thousands of children like he'd been—poor, from homes with one parent or being raised by someone other than their parent, forgotten—and to give them opportunities to be something more than what society or a deprived community branded them to be. If not for football and attentive, encouraging coaches, he would've never reached college, much less the NFL.

Many of these kids would most likely not have the same NFL career as him, Dom, or Ronin. But those skills could help them earn scholarships to colleges. Help them receive a degree that would pave the way for a successful future they'd never dreamed themselves capable of achieving.

He glanced across the local high school field where the camp was held. At least one hundred and twenty-five boys in purple or gold jerseys congregated in specialized groups running individual and team drills or receiving one-on-one training on the field with the staff. Several players, including Ronin and Dom, as well as guys he'd played with at LSU who'd gone on to professional football careers, had volunteered their time. As did a few high school, college, and even a couple of NFL coaches.

He was proud. And if his grandmother was here, she would be, too.

He squinted at the current 7-on-7 drill between the offensive line—quarterback, running back, and receivers—against the defensive backs. The thirteen-year-old from Kalamazoo, Michigan, playing quarterback had a good arm. Great actually. He launched the ball in a tight spiral, and the kid playing wide receiver made a beautiful catch. They ran the drill again, and Zeph couldn't help noticing the boy playing his position, tight end. Fifteen, one hundred and ninety pounds, and already six feet, Tyler Jackson from Baton Rouge reminded Zeph of himself at that age. The boy had speed, great hands, and could block his ass off. And a chip on his shoulder the size of Lake Ponchartrain. Not surprising considering his rough background. No father in the picture, drug-addicted mother, foster home after foster home. If not for his incredible athleticism, he could have easily become a statistic. All the things that marked him as troubled in society's eyes made him perfect for the Jaybird Foundation.

Blowing his whistle to stop the play, Zeph strode onto the field.

"Tyler, you cut the route off." When the boy frowned, Zeph didn't take offense, just explained. "You should've run ten yards instead of eight before you made the cut. You would've had more depth in the route." Moving to the line of scrimmage, he demonstrated for the teen, and the frown cleared, replaced by understanding. Taking a couple more minutes, he worked with Tyler, letting him run the route before Zeph reclaimed his place on the sideline.

About a half-hour later, they stopped for a short break, and that's when he felt her. He didn't have to turn around to know Sophia had arrived. It was funny how he'd stopped thinking of her as Giovanna; it hadn't been difficult. Except for the photo shoot, the woman he'd spent time with had little in common with the model he'd met a year ago. She could've been two different people.

Pivoting, he scanned the bleachers bordering the field, and seconds later, spotted her. Though she wore sunglasses, that blue-tipped hair—today in a partial top knot with the rest of those gorgeous, thick waves flowing over her shoulders—was a dead giveaway. Before he was even conscious of moving, his feet moved in her direction.

"Zeph," a voice carrying the Southern accent of his home called out.

Gritting his teeth, he halted, though every sense, every damn cell in his body, vibrated with the need to get to Sophia. Find out her answer. Determine if she would be under him, in his bed, tonight. Discover if she would let him inside her again.

Instead, he waited, turning slightly as his ex-girlfriend, Shalene Gallow, approached him.

It'd been two years since their breakup—since she'd broken his heart and trust after revealing how deceitful and disloyal she was—but there was one area of his life where he hadn't been able to kick her out. She'd been instrumental in helping him establish the foundation five years ago. For all her faults, the purpose and mission of the organization had been close to her heart. She had grown up in a single-family home like Zeph, raised by her mother. While Shalene had been an honor student and gifted singer, her brother had chosen the path many other young black men in their community had. Drug dealing, gang-banging. And at nineteen, he'd paid the ultimate price with his life, devastating his family, and especially Shalene, who'd hero-worshipped her older brother.

Shalene had been passionate about three things: fame, Zeph's money, and offering young men another choice besides the one that had led to her brother's death. So even when they had broken up, he couldn't take her position at the foundation away from her. Besides, as her handling of the day-to-day activities and special field trips exhibited, she excelled as the foundation's community outreach coordinator. It would've been a case of cutting off his nose to spite his face if he'd fired her.

And besides, Shalene had a child to provide for and raise.

A child that wasn't his.

Just the thought of the toddler with the tight cap of black curls and dark brown eyes had a knife of pain stabbing between his ribs. Deliberately, he shoved the image of the boy safely behind the mental vault door he'd labeled Don't Fuck With, and focused on the woman before him.

So he'd kept Shalene on. Still...Josephine Black hadn't raised a fool. Zeph had an independent accounting firm as well as the CFO handling the funds, not his ex. If their relationship had revealed one thing to him, it was Shalene couldn't be trusted around money.

"I've been trying to catch you all day," she said, the strides of her long legs bared by white shorts closing the distance between them. She smiled, and at one time, the expression on her beautiful face would've won her anything she asked of him. Now he just wondered what agenda the smile hid. With sheer determination, he prevented the bitterness of the thought from coloring his voice or expression. "The camp has been absolutely wonderful so far."

"Yeah, it has," he agreed. "You needed something?"

The grin dimmed a bit at his abruptness. "I just wanted to know if you had some time to go over the schedule for tomorrow for the field trip to CenturyLink Field." She laid a hand on his forearm. "It was awesome of your coach to arrange a tour of where the Warriors play. I know the kids are going to love it."

Zeph nodded, forcing his body not to tense under her touch. Coach Declan had definitely come through, and he'd already overheard some of the boys talking about the trip. "Thanks for handling the details and preparations for tomorrow."

Not only were the teens visiting where Zeph, Dom, and Ronin played, but they would have the afternoon off at Wild Waves Theme and Water Park.

"Of course." She squeezed his arm. "You know I love doing this. I was hoping we could discuss plans and everything over dinner tonight?" She shifted closer to him, tipping her head back. "I would love to cook for you. I called Mama last night to get her special bread pudding recipe to go along with my seafood gumbo."

The invitation in her gaze didn't include only food. In the past, they wouldn't have made it to dinner. Would've eaten it much later in bed after sex. But that was then. And today, the offer left him cold. No, that wasn't totally accurate. To say it left him cold meant he didn't feel anything, was numb. And he was far from numb when it came to his ex. Where she used to stir pleasure and joy within him, now she caused anger and resentment to fill his chest.

"I have plans, sorry." Yeah, not really. "But text me with whatever questions or concerns you have about tomorrow, and we'll address them early in the morning."

He didn't wait for her response but turned and resumed his trek toward Sophia and away from the wreckage of his past. He couldn't help comparing the two women along the way. Both were beautiful, but Giovanna was a successful model, had a career of her own, and as far as he could see, she didn't depend on someone else to hand it to her—while Shalene had used Zeph's reputation and job to catapult her to fame. She'd even tried to rope him into participating on one of those fucking reality shows. His answer had been a resounding hell no.

Sophia could be endearingly sweet, as her nervous babbling about *St. Elmo's Fire* had shown. And in the next breath, blunt and uninhibited with her passion. Even her insistence on time to consider the "arrangement" he'd proposed had struck him as honest. But if his ex had taught him anything, it was not to accept anything at face value. He'd believed Shalene to be the same loving girl she'd been in high school, but she'd proved herself to be the definition of deceit. It might be cynical that a part of him waited for Sophia to follow in Shalene's footsteps, but it would also be foolish if it didn't.

He climbed the bleachers until he reached Sophia, now joined by Tennyson. As Dom's PA as well as best friend, she could usually be found wherever the quarterback was. Both women smiled at him, but it was Sophia's—with delight and a hint of shyness—that sent heat rolling through him, rivalling the warmth of the day.

"I'm glad you made it," he greeted her, taking in the body-hugging white tank top and loose, cotton pants she wore. How could she make simple, everyday clothes as tantalizing as the sexiest lingerie? It was a mystery up there with the Sphinx and the Madden Curse.

He'd intended to sit down and talk to her, spend the break trying to figure out where her head was. But one look at her—at her smooth, olive skin that damn near shone in the sun; at the pretty mouth that had been sliding down his chest last night in a particularly hot dream; at the firm, beautiful breasts that his palms itched to cup—and all of his intentions snapped like a dry rubber band.

Clasping her hand in his, he tugged her to her feet. "Hey, Tenny," he said to his friend as he guided Sophia down the bleachers.

"Hi." A smile quirked the corner of her mouth. "Bye."

"Zephirin," Sophia muttered from behind him, poking him in the back with her free hand. "What are you doing?"

Rather than answer, he led her away from the field and toward the entrance to the locker rooms. Other than pausing to hold the heavy door open for her, he didn't stop until they reached the abandoned girls' locker room. He twisted the lock behind them and immediately turned and pushed her against the wall.

"Five days," he complained, lust roughening his voice. Cupping her face, he tilted her head back, rubbed his mouth across hers. Groaned. "I tried giving you space to think, but…"

He didn't finish the sentence…couldn't. On the tail of another groan, he covered her mouth with his, taking the kiss he'd been denied for so long. *Goddamn*. She tasted as sweet, *better*, than he remembered. Hunger rode him, and he claimed her like a starving man. His tongue thrust past her parted lips, demanding she give him what he needed—her passion, her surrender. And after a pause so brief he wouldn't have detected it if he wasn't so hyper-aware of everything about her, she gave it to him.

Her surrender, her taste—it beat back the past and its dark memories like the sun banishing the stain of shadows. Here, pressed against her body, her flavor filling him, thoughts of lies, pain, betrayal, and a kid who should've been his but wasn't, disappeared. Leaving only Sophia.

Her fingers cuffed his wrists, and she opened her mouth wider without him asking. She curled her tongue around his, sucking it like she'd done to his fingers Friday night, and the pull arrowed straight to his dick. God, she was a drug. Suddenly, he understood why the addicts in his neighborhood risked everything to chase that high. It was a ravenous emptiness that couldn't be satisfied. But the trying...the trying was nirvana.

He released her face but not her mouth. Skimming his fingers down her neck, he paused to press his thumbs over her pulse. Enjoyed the rapid drum of it. Loved knowing he caused it. Dipping his head, he tongued the hollow and vein that telegraphed her arousal. A whimper escaped her, and damn if that wasn't his new favorite sound. Well, other than the choked cry she made when coming.

Giving her neck one last lick, he trailed his lips over her collarbone, smoothed his hands down her shoulders and cupped her breasts. Finally.

"We shouldn't. Not here..." She uttered the protest, but the grip on his head belied the breathy tone. "Zephirin," she repeated, twisting into his caress. "God. Please."

He loved that she said his whole name. Everyone else he knew—and even those he didn't—called him by the shortened version. But his given name in her husky, made-for-sex voice was a stroke to his senses. He wanted to hear it again. And again. He reached down and grasped the hem of her top, tugged it up. Jerked one of the cups of her black bra down.

"*Jesus Christ,*" he rasped.

Pierced. Sophia's nipple was goddamned pierced.

Stunned, he somehow found the strength and will to drag his eyes from the most erotic, carnal sight he'd ever seen. The small silver ring with the tiny ball in the middle hadn't been there the other night. He damn sure would've remembered it.

He glanced up at her, and she must've read the question and healthy dose of *what the hell?* on his face because she flushed, her tongue peeking out to dampen her lips. "I, uh, removed them along with my other piercings for the shoot."

"You are sexy as fuck," he growled. Pinching the little hoop, he lightly tugged, and stared, utterly enraptured as she cried out, her back arching into a tight bow. "Does it hurt?" Though lust snarled and snapped at him to get on with it, he hesitated, needing to know her limitations. The thought of inadvertently causing her pain was the only thing that could halt the onslaught of want pouring through him like a raging, swollen river.

"Yes, n-no," she stammered, shaking her head. "Both. Do it again."

Before the last word left her mouth, he sucked her nipple between his lips. He swirled his tongue around the tip, licking, stroking. Her fingernails bit his scalp, and the minute pricks of pain spurred him on, sent blood pounding like a primal drum in his cock. He drew harder on her, capturing the piece of jewelry between his teeth and pulling. She shuddered against him, her body like a dancing flame beneath his hands and mouth as she twisted and writhed. Her low pleas and whimpers teased his ears, each greedy sound a reward.

He released her flesh with a soft pop and a last lick. Anticipation riding him, he yanked down the other cup and discovered a twin piercing in the other nipple. On a harsh curse, he lowered his head and curled his tongue around the hardened bead, rolling the other wet peak between his fingers. He could've easily spent the rest of the afternoon tasting her breasts, playing with the exotic jewelry that turned him on like nothing else. Just when he believed he had a handle on who she was, she kept surprising him. Delighting him.

Tearing his mouth away from her, he trailed a path down the center of her chest, over her belly and the green gem nestled just inside her navel. For some inexplicable—and inexcusable—reason, he'd missed it when dragging up her shirt.

Huffing out a low chuckle, he swiftly tongued her flesh and the jewelry. "Anything else I need to know about?" he rumbled, shooting a quick look up her torso.

"No," she said, a flash of humor entering those chocolate eyes alongside the lust. "I'm too chicken for the last one."

"Somehow I doubt you're scared of anything," he murmured, stroking her hips.

Once again, something glimmered in her gaze, but this time he couldn't decipher it. The emotion disappeared under her lowered lashes. "You scare me," she replied, voice so soft he almost didn't catch it.

"Why?" He brushed his lips over the smooth, tender skin above the waistband of her loose cotton pants. But he didn't go any further, waiting for her answer.

She inhaled, and the breath escaped her on a delicate shudder that reverberated through the body he cradled in his hands. "You make me want things I shouldn't. That I know better than to take. Wanting you makes me selfish."

The honesty in the bare naked statement tackled him harder than the most hyped up defensive back. As did the hint of something darker. *Guilt? Remorse?* The insidious voice whispered against his skull. But he pushed the thought away. It didn't have a place here between them. Not with her beautiful, pierced breasts bared, and her sex only inches away from him.

"Be selfish then, baby." With hands harder than he intended, he jerked down the pants, taking her underwear with them. He shoved the clothes down her legs, revealing her to him. Ignoring her gasp, he cupped a thigh and hiked it over his shoulder, opening her before him. For him. "You want permission? Fine. I give it to you."

He put his mouth on her.

Her cry bounced off the walls of the vacant locker room, and he groaned against her flesh. *Damn*, the taste of her. Sweet like the fruit and flowers scent of her skin, except heavier, thicker, with a musk that was all woman. All her.

More. The demand beat against his skull, and he surrendered to it without hesitation. He licked a path down her slit, pausing to nip at each fold before tonguing the clenching entrance to her body. Tilting his head, he spread her wide and drove inside her. As far as he could, enjoying the fluttering of her feminine muscles as they tried to grasp onto him. On a growl, he withdrew, plunged. Withdrew, plunged. Unable to stop. To get enough.

She rocked her hips against him, her hands holding his head in a vise grip. With an abandon that had his cock as solid as a steel pipe, she rode his mouth, an endless stream of words falling from her in a dirty, desperate litany. One stroke of his fist, that's all it would take to explode. But that would mean releasing her. And that he wasn't willing to do.

Running the flat of his tongue over her folds, he returned to the top of her sex and the pulsing, pink flesh that had his damn mouth watering for a taste. He flicked the engorged nub, teasing it, playing with it. Her half groan, half wail telegraphed her need, her frustration. Yeah, he would've loved to push her, string her on the taut edge of release without letting her fall over. But he didn't have time, and frankly, not the patience. He craved her orgasm like it was his own. Couldn't deny her.

Shifting one hand lower and the other higher, he thrust two fingers inside her and pinched her nipple and tugged on her piercing. And sucked hard on her clit.

She went off like a bomb.

Growling against her flesh, he continued thrusting, tugging and sucking. Drawing out her pleasure. Giving her every measure of it.

Only when she fell limp against the wall, their breath rough and harsh in the silence of the room, did he release her. He replaced her pants and underwear, and rising to his feet, adjusted her bra and shirt.

He stretched his arms and flattened his palms on the wall, placing her curves out of reach and granting him time to regain his tattered control. To cool down his body that ached with the need to be balls-deep in her.

"What's your answer?" he ground out, wishing he could gentle his voice, but with lust a pissed-off animal howling inside him, it proved an impossibility. "Are you going to let me have you? Are you going to take me?"

Her long, dark lashes lifted. The passion hadn't evaporated from her gaze, but there was clarity there. Enough that when she whispered, "Yes," his fingers curled against the wall in a fist in triumph.

"Stay," he said, surprising himself. This thing between them was sex only and temporary. It didn't include inviting her into his world, or him visiting hers. And yet, with the reminder a loud echo in his head, he didn't rescind the offer.

Some kind of struggle waged across her expressive face, but finally, she nodded. "Okay."

Risking a brush of his lips over hers, he pulled back before temptation could reel him in and make him later returning to the field than he already was. But, even as he enfolded her hand in his and led her from the locker room, he couldn't evict the niggling kernel of unease in his head.

He had to remember the boundaries he'd set. That forgive-and-forget bullshit was for naive assholes.

He couldn't *afford* to forget.

Chapter Eleven

"To paraphrase Vivian Ward, the winsome, kind-hearted prostitute from *Pretty Woman*, the whole seduction thing is nice, but here's a tip: I'm a sure thing." Sophia perched on the edge of the leather bucket seat, trying not to stare through the glass floor to Elliot Bay about two hundred feet below.

After camp ended, Zephirin had taken her out to dinner, and she'd let it slip that she'd never been on Seattle's iconic Great Wheel, a huge observation Ferris wheel on Pier 57. He'd insisted on introducing her to it, complete with a VIP package that included a private ride in a luxury "gondola," a special VIP T-shirt, photo book pictures, and champagne that they'd both passed on. Him, because of training, and her because she'd never really cared for the fizzy wine. The whole thing smacked of "date night," and it made her uncomfortable. Dating wasn't part of their arrangement. Sex. Hot, Raiders-of-the-Lost-Ark-Face-Melting sex was included in their deal. Not gorgeous, breathtaking views of the bay, city skyline, Mount Rainier, and Olympic Mountains. Not romance.

For five days, she'd argued and haggled with herself about

taking Zephirin up on his offer. And she'd allowed herself to give in, to take what she craved with a hunger usually reserved for salted caramel, if she followed two stipulations: keep it about sex, and end it on Sunday before Giovanna returns home.

Then he'd gone down on her in an empty locker room, turning her into a woman who had mind-altering Bill Clinton Sex in public places, and escorted her on a date.

God, she had the spine of a jellyfish. A jellyfish suffering from scoliosis.

"This isn't seduction; this is me giving you something you haven't experienced yet. It's what friends do."

"Not friends who fuck," she grumbled under her breath.

"Even friends who fuck." Without warning, a large pair of hands gripped her waist and planted her on his lap. Before she could shriek a protest, his arm circled her lower back, and the other stretched across her thighs, holding her close to his wide, hard chest. She forced herself to remain upright and not recline against that huge expanse of muscle that seemed to beckon her. "And if I were seducing you, I would do this..." He nuzzled the skin behind her ear—a previously unknown erogenous zone with a mainline to her clit and the breasts he'd been so fascinated with earlier in the locker room. "And this." He slid a hand up her leg and wedged it between her thighs, cupping her. Her body went from simmering to flash fire in zero-point-two seconds. "And tell you that I can't get your sweet taste out of my mouth. Can't erase the sounds of you coming out of my head. Can't wait to watch you sink down on my cock, while I play with those pretty nipple piercings again as you take me inside."

Molten lava replaced her blood, and she was half surprised she didn't exhale plumes of smoke. Stunned and so turned on, she turned her head, checking out the smoky-tinted windows of the gondola to determine if they would give Seattle and God a show if she straddled him right there on the Great Wheel.

She cleared her throat. Fought not to fidget on his lap. "Then I guess it's a good thing you're not trying to seduce me." When his low chuckle reverberated in her ear, she scrambled for a safer topic. Anything to divert her attention from the fireworks snap, crackle, popping in her panties. "Tell me something about yourself," she blurted, picking up the conversation they'd started in his kitchen the previous Friday. "Why football? You seem so different from other players that if I'd met you on the street, I wouldn't have guessed you played the sport. You're calmer, quieter, smarter...kinder."

He studied her for a long, silent moment. "And you know a lot of football players?"

She shrugged, now wishing she'd kept the last part to herself. As her statement replayed in her head, it sounded biased at best, insulting at worst. "A few. From high school. They were complete assholes." The words slipped past her lips without her conscious permission. But once she started, she couldn't seem to stop. To stem the flow. "They were loud, obnoxious, cruel..."

"Bullies," Zephirin quietly interjected. "They bullied you, Sophia?"

"Yes." Releasing a sigh, she tried to rise from his lap, but his arms tightened, holding her in place. Rubbing a hand over her bare arms, she shook her head. "I know it's silly to stereotype a group because of my experiences with a few people. It's been years since I graduated high school. Years since I was tormented daily for the crimes of being different, shy, and insecure. It's not like it was just the jocks. Others joined in, but the athletes—the gods of our school— were the ringleaders. Especially if my sister rejected one of their advances, then I often received the brunt of their embarrassment and anger. For me, high school was hell. It's

why I chose the peacock for a tattoo, not because it's pretty."
She shook her head, remembering the lame excuse she'd given
him the night they met. "The peacock symbolizes renewal,
awakening, guidance, and protection. It reminds me of where
I was and how far I've come." She huffed out a part-mortified
laugh, fixing her gaze on the icy peak of Mount Rainier.
"God, I'm sorry. I must sound so pathetic. Good thing this
isn't a date, huh?" she teased, trying to cover for unloading
her emotional shit all over Zephirin and Elliott Bay.

"Look at me." The command came seconds before a
hand stroked up her back and tunneled into her hair, ensuring
she obeyed. She met his gold and green eyes, bracing herself
for any wisp of pity. And almost wilted in relief when she
didn't find it. "Never apologize for the inexcusable, abusive
actions of other people. You might've gone through hell,
but you came out strong. Beautiful. The toughest, most
indestructible swords are forged in the hottest fires. And the
longer they remain in, the more resilient and shatterproof
they are. That's you. Let me put it in terms you understand.
What's that sword the king in *Lord of the Rings* carried? The
one that elf brought back to him? You're that sword. Broken.
Remade. Indestructible."

Well, hell.

Tears stung her eyes, and she quickly batted her lashes,
willing them away. He'd called her Andúril, Aragorn's sword.
That had to be the absolute sweetest compliment she'd
received. Ever.

"Catering to my nerdy heart will get you everything,"
she said, once she was able to speak past the fist of emotion
squeezing her throat. "Now, back to my original question.
Football. Why?"

"I love it," he stated. His hand massaged her scalp,
and she worked to focus on his explanation instead of purr
like a contented kitten. "It saved my life. As dramatic as

it sounds, it's also true. I grew up in Little Woods, a rough neighborhood in New Orleans. Drugs, gangs, murders—I was surrounded by it. And as wonderful as my grandmother was, it would've been so easy to fall into all that. But in seventh grade, my social studies teacher, who also happened to be the school's football coach, recruited me. I learned I had options if I worked hard enough. It offered me, and ultimately, my family, a way out."

He tipped his head back against the seat, staring at the top of the gondola.

"But, also, I just love the sport. It's the ultimate high and challenge. Pitting your strength, mind, and will against another man. The adrenaline. The rush. It's a battle, victory, pain, pleasure, hate, love, fear, faith. All rolled into one. The first time I stepped on that field when I was twelve, I suddenly understood what my grandmother felt when she entered a church. I didn't want to stop playing. And I haven't yet."

She blinked, the utter passion in his voice stealing her breath. To her, the game had always seemed like men in pads and uniforms running a ball up and down a field in the most brutal and confusing manner possible. But listening to him... She understood in that moment, that for Zephirin, the sport was a part of him, had fashioned him as surely as her experiences—good and bad—had shaped her. For that, she might just have to fall in love with the game.

Fall in love.

She inched back from those three words like a leery jumper creeping back from a crumbling ledge. She should never, *ever* think, much less speak, those words in connection with Zephirin. Only bad things led down that road.

"Speaking of football," she hedged, pushing out of his embrace, and squelching the disappointment over him letting her go. She shifted to the seat beside him, and nerves took flight in her stomach like a flock of startled birds. A big-ass flock. Maybe she should forget it. It was probably a bad idea, and it wasn't like he'd asked for her opinion...

"Speaking of football?" he prompted with an arched eyebrow.

Screw it. What the hell? "Have you ever considered creating an app for your foundation and football program?"

"We have one," he said. Paused. "You looked up the foundation?"

The blush crept up her chest and poured into her face before she could prevent it. "I had to do something while I waited for you this afternoon. Unlike you, football is an enigma to me. So, yes, I did a little research. Anyway..." She glanced away from his piercing stare. "I saw you have one where people can receive updates about the foundation and track your appearances and events. But I'm talking about something more interactive. Something more...fun. No offense."

"None taken," he replied, nodding. "What were you thinking?"

"Well..." She curled a leg under her hips, turning to more fully face him as she warmed up to the subject. "I saw on your website that competition to register for your camp is fierce. The kids need recommendations, have to write essays, etc., and the process starts fairly early in the year."

"True," he agreed. "One of our mottos is nothing worth having comes easy. So they have to work for entrance. Because of the stipulations, registration opens in November and notifications go out in January."

"I also noticed today that the kids were split into two teams, yellow and purple—"

"Gold."

She drew up short at the interruption. "Huh?"

"Gold," he corrected. "Not yellow."

Exasperated, she waved a hand. "Yellow, gold. What's

the difference?"

"There's a difference. Gold," he ground out.

Huffing out a breath, she barely managed not to roll her eyes. "Fine. They were split into two teams. *Gold* and purple. I'm guessing most of the kids don't meet until they arrive at camp? What if, to build team spirit or camaraderie, you create an app for the kids that connect them to their team members early on? They can see the roster of who they're playing with, maybe contact them through profiles. But also, they could start competing before they arrive at camp. Each player can win points that contribute to the overall score of their team. They can earn points by keeping their grades up, doing chores, reading books, excelling on the football field, community service, just to name a few."

She leaned forward, her nervousness forgotten as she explained the idea that had come to her that afternoon. "And their parents, teachers, and coaches would have access to the app as well so they could enter grades, accomplishments, and praise. The team score could be announced at camp, and those kids would receive a special gift. Like an afternoon with their favorite player. Or specially designed and autographed merchandise. Sponsors would jump to endorse and fund this kind of app for the attention and promotion it would bring them. I think…"

Her voice trailed off. Zephirin stared at her, his expression inscrutable. He didn't move, as still as a statue.

The worry returned full-fledged, and she wished it was possible to kick one's own ass. "I'm sorry," she murmured. "I overstepped. It's your charity. I didn't mean to—"

"It's brilliant."

The low, fervent reply took her aback. For several seconds, she floundered, caught between shock, relief, and delight. "Really?" She grinned. "It's a big project, but I think the sponsorships and endorsements alone would fund not only the development, but help the foundation, too. And you can always incorporate ads into it..." Her mind flew ahead, analyzing certain aspects.

"How do you know about apps? What gave you the idea for one?"

Every thought, every movement, every breath halted. Ice that tasted of fear slid through her veins. She'd slipped; she'd been so excited about the idea that she hadn't considered what it might reveal. Damn.

Tell him the truth. The soft voice of her conscience whispered through her head, and she parted her lips, about to spill it all.

But at the last second, caution slammed into her with all the subtlety of a brick. All the reasons she'd remained silent about her identity still held true. More than ever now. Giovanna's reputation and career. And given Zephirin's demand for honesty between them, if he discovered she'd been lying to him from the moment they met, she suspected his anger would be terrible. There would be no reason for him not to tell *Sports Unlimited* about their charade. When others had given in, Giovanna had worked and struggled to obtain her success. Sophia couldn't jeopardize it.

And then the fact remained that he would want nothing to do with her, of course. And selfishly—so fucking selfishly—she wanted these next few days with him. She'd eventually have to confess, but was it wrong to want to wring out just a little more time with him before he hated the sight of her?

Be selfish then, baby. You want permission? Fine. I give it to you.

He'd said those words to her earlier, assuaging her guilt if even for that time in the locker room. But there was no erasing the burden of her lies. She had to carry it, face the consequences when the time came. But that time wasn't now.

"My sister is an app developer," she lied. Again. The

untruth sat on her tongue like ash, dirtying her.

"Right. You mentioned having a sister earlier." As if remembering the context in which she'd revealed a sibling, he reached for her hand, smoothed his thumb over the backs of her fingers. "Is she good?"

"She thinks so." Sophia smiled, wondering if it appeared as wry as it felt. "Her career is like what football means to you—her passion." Talking about herself in the third person was weird and disconcerting. But she couldn't stop, because she needed him to know even a little about the *real* her. "Ever since we were kids, computers, how they operated, their programming, fascinated her. Like you said football saved you... I think it did the same for her. Gave her a safe, non-judgmental place to land."

"Was she bullied, too?"

Sophia glanced away. "Only one of us was," she murmured.

He didn't press her any further on the sensitive subject, but he covered her hand with his and rubbed soothing circles over her knuckles with his thumb. The gesture was meant to bring comfort—and it did. But as she stared at that big hand damn near swallowing hers, she couldn't help but remember how his body had covered her smaller one. That quickly, the warmth sliding through her heated, and it had as much to do with his gentle reassurance as the erotic image playing front and center in her head.

"You think your sister would be interested in developing the app for my foundation? Or at least taking a look at the idea?"

Excitement and joy bubbled up inside her chest. Bringing to fruition a project she'd conceived especially for him? *Yes!* The shout echoed inside her head, but right on the heels of the last reverberation, reality intruded with a slap that left her ears ringing.

Sophia Cruz couldn't have anything to do with the Jaybird Foundation—or Zephirin Black—after Sunday.

Delight seeped out of her like a slow-leaking balloon. With herculean effort, she prevented her face from betraying the tangle of emotions inside of her. "She's not a freelancer; she works for a sports-related company, so I'm not sure if there would be a non-compete issue."

"Does she want to work for herself?" he asked.

"*Yes.*" No way could she keep the hope, fear, and passion out of her answer. Not when the truth tore out of her like a tornado. What would it feel like to be open with him? To share her dreams, desires, and frustrations with him? To not have this Damocles Sword of him finding out the truth swinging over her head?

Launching to her feet, she crossed the small distance to the tinted glass. Like a hamster trapped in a constantly moving wheel, she ached with the need to get off this ride of lies. To escape the suffocating weight of it, and just *be* with him.

Be her, even if the real her wasn't quite up to his standards.

Be true.

Be honest.

It clawed at her, the need pressing down on her from not just all sides, but from inside.

I don't need feelings—I don't want them... Don't muddy it up with anything deeper than sex and orgasms... If whatever you plan on telling me will make this deeper than it needs to be and prevent me from taking you, then let it go.

His words echoed in her head. They both liberated her from and chained her to the lie.

When the gondola finally slowed and halted, she beat Zephirin to the opening. Air. She needed air. And not the one saturated with her deception.

Stepping off, she practically ran from the ride and long

line of people waiting for their turn on the tourist attraction. With his long legs, Zephirin had no problem keeping up with her pace. And by the time they reached the parking garage and his black Escalade, her heart pumped as if she'd sprinted the quarter mile. He, however, didn't appear in the least winded.

Silently, he opened the passenger door and guided her in. Seconds later when he settled behind the steering wheel, the disquieting, almost feverish sense of time not slipping but plummeting away hadn't eased.

Grab every minute. Savor it. Hoard it.

The commands, edged in the desperation that seethed inside her like a boiling cauldron, pushed at her mind as she snapped her seat belt in place.

Beside her, Zephirin fit the key in the ignition. She shot her hand out, gripping his. He glanced at her, his gaze inscrutable.

"Fuck me."

Chapter Twelve

Zephirin didn't move, but her whispered half demand, half plea slammed into him, pummeling the air from his frozen lungs. Hearing "fuck" on her lips had the same effect of a fist to his cock. His body roared, "Hell yes!" but his mind—the part not hijacked by lust—realized something was…off. Had been since leaving the Great Wheel. Actually, before then. Right after she'd shared her wonderful idea about an app for the kids attending his camp. The band that had tightened around him still hadn't fully loosened. That she cared enough about his vision, his foundation and the boys to come up with that inspired concept… If possible, it had ratcheted his lust for her higher.

But as much as he wanted to give her exactly what she requested of him, he couldn't ignore the indecipherable emotion darkening her eyes from brown to almost black.

He twisted in his seat and cupped the back of her neck. "What's wrong?" he asked. Funny how they'd known each other only a handful of days, and he could read her more easily than he ever could Shalene in the four years they'd been together. Either Sophia really was as honest as she portrayed, or she was just a better actress than his ex. "And don't tell me nothing."

Releasing her seat belt, she shot across the console, crushing her mouth to his. On instinct, he parted his lips, welcoming the thrust of her tongue, encouraging the tight hold on his head by threading his fingers through her hair and pressing the tips into her scalp. For a long moment, he drowned in her sultry taste, the hungry tangle of tongues, the greedy gasps and whimpers. But after one last lick to the roof of her mouth, he tugged on her hair, pulling her mouth away.

"Tell me," he ordered.

She pressed her forehead to his, her breath shuddering over his lips. "I don't want to talk about it. Not now. Just..." She gave him a short, almost chaste kiss. "Please, make me forget for a little while, okay?"

Part of him wanted to deliver a flat no, force her back to the passenger seat, and push her to spill the truth so he could fix whatever put the shadows in her eyes. Be her personal Warrior, not just Washington's. But the other half...that half couldn't deny her anything...

When his ex had used him, he'd resented her for it. Hell, still did. But letting Sophia use his body to give herself oblivion, even if for a little while, wasn't a betrayal. It was a pleasure.

Instead of replying, he silently thanked God for dark tinted windows, shoved his seat back, and lowered it to a half-reclining position. Raising his arms, he grabbed the headrest behind him, relating to her without words that she could have him. Have whatever she needed.

She stared at him, unmoving. Then, with a sound that could've been either a cry or a groan—maybe both—she slid her hands under his T-shirt, smoothing her palms up his stomach and chest. He gritted his teeth when her fingers skimmed his nipples, the electric shock of her touch sizzling in his veins. When the material bunched at his shoulders, she gripped it, and he allowed her to lift it over his head and settle the shirt in back of his neck.

"Beautiful," she softly praised, climbing over the console and straddling him.

It wasn't the first, or even hundredth, time he'd been on the receiving end of that particular compliment. But from her? Given the pleasure humming beneath his skin, he could've been hearing it for the first time.

Before he had a chance to respond, she pressed down on him, circling those feminine, created-for-his-hands hips, stroking her sex over his cock. Even through his jeans and her pants, he could feel her, that hot, wet flesh that he'd had his mouth on hours earlier.

"Again," he ground out, his jaw tight. "Do it again."

Stretching her arms up, she curled her fingers over the headrest, just inside his hands. Ducking her head, she opened her mouth over his neck as she undulated against him, her thighs squeezing him. Damn, he could come like this—like a teenager frantically humping and grinding with his girlfriend in the backseat of his car.

His breath caught at "girlfriend."

That's not what this is, logic that hadn't yet been swamped by lust cautioned. *Remember this is temporary, has an expiration date. We don't do—*

The rest of that warning splintered under her tongue lashing his nipple. He groaned, arching under her, almost unseating her. He clung harder to the seat, but when her teeth raked him, he swore, gripped her hair and pressed her to him, demanding she repeat the caress. She brought tongue, lips, and teeth into play, toying with him, torturing him. With each suck and lick, each roll of her hips, the temperature in his body rocketed, the mercury simmering on high.

She switched to his other nipple, and he couldn't help but wonder if this was payback for earlier. If so, he verged on pleading with her to continue punishing him. Her teeth captured his flesh and tugged, and his cock thumped as if the caress had been delivered to it. Both of his hands were in her hair now, and when she flicked him with her tongue for the last time before slipping down his body, he almost dragged her back up. But this was about her, what she needed. So he gritted his teeth and held on.

Her tongue followed the tattoos inked into his chest and stomach. Her hum of pleasure vibrated against his skin seconds before her tongue traced every ridge of his abdomen. In that moment, he'd never been so glad he took the utmost care of his body. Before now, he would've attributed his strict, regimented routine to his career. But with her paying homage to him with her mouth, football had suddenly become the second reason. Her appreciation, that second moan of delight, had supplanted it.

Fumbling fingers tugged at his belt, and his stomach went concave under the grazing touch. Shit. She didn't intend…

"Sophia," he said, the sound serrated and harsh in the heavy silence. "Baby, you don't have to…" The protest died as she wiggled further down his body, settling between his spread legs and the steering wheel. Quickly, she released the button on his jeans and lowered the zipper.

"I know I don't have to." She dipped her hand in the waistband of his boxer briefs. Her breath broke on the tense air. "I *want* to."

Her fist closed around his cock. Squeezed. And his long, low moan filled the car. He bucked into her grip, no control over his hips. He'd become her instrument to play, her shot to call. He lifted his ass off the seat, shoved his jeans and boxers further down so she could have free rein over him. She thanked him with another slow, hard pump of his dick. From base to tip, she stroked him. And he shuddered and rocked into her hand.

"Tell me what you like," she murmured, her breath a soft, heated caress over his taut skin. Another ripple of lust worked its way through his body. Both at the sensual command and the almost touch of her mouth.

"Harder," he directed. "Squeeze me harder. You won't hurt me."

She immediately complied, her fist clamping tighter, the slide down his flesh rougher. His balls drew up against him, electrical currents building, building...

Then she sucked him.

"Fuck," he hissed. He launched up from the seat, sitting straight up as a dark snarl reverberated in his chest. *Have to see. Need to see.*

The words chanted in his head like a carnal mantra as he took in her lush, full lips parted around his cock, taking him inside, welcoming him into the warm, wet haven that was both heaven and hell.

"Jesus Christ, that's pretty," he rasped, one hand buried in the thick, blue-tipped brown strands, and the other clutching the handlebar above him. He couldn't remove his gaze from her. Her lashes fluttered down, shielding her eyes from him, but not the expression of hunger that suffused her face. The need she didn't try to hide. Lust barreled through him, hardening his flesh even more.

She explored him. Leisurely. Slowly. Painfully. He inhaled deep, wielding control over his body, forcing it to remain still, letting her take him how she wanted. But damn... He closed his eyes, only to open them seconds later at the flutter of her tongue directly beneath his crown. Fire blazed down his spine, and it snapped the tattered, steadily unraveling ropes that had been holding him down.

"Suck it, baby. Take me deeper," he growled, his hold

on her head tensing, not leaving any room for argument. Fortunately, she didn't seem inclined to disagree, instead parting her lips wider and allowing him to push more of himself inside. "That's it," he praised, careful not to rush her. Letting her become accustomed to his length.

But she didn't want his tenderness. Her tongue swirled around him, her mouth wrapping as tight as the fist still closed around the thickest, widest part of him. Raising higher on her knees, she took him down, down, until the head of his cock bumped the back of her throat. As she withdrew, her moan vibrated along his erection, adding another sensory caress. She didn't hold back; her head bobbed up and down, letting him slide into the narrow opening of her throat. He choked back a shout, tugging her head up, her mouth off him.

She stared up at him, eyes glazed, features soft with arousal, lips damp from the best blow job of his existence.

"Get up here," he snarled.

"Not yet," she objected, her hand sliding up and down his dick. "Not until you come."

"I will," he said, cupping her under the shoulders and dragging her back onto his lap. "Just not here." He crashed his mouth to hers, uncaring that he'd just been there. On the contrary, he fucking thrilled in it. "Here." He palmed her between the legs, and her thighs closed around his hand. "Now get those pants off."

This time she didn't argue with him. She lifted her hips and stripped off her pants while he removed a condom from his back pocket and pushed his jeans further down. He bracketed her waist, holding her as she shifted and resumed her perch on top of him. Briefly closing his eyes as her bare skin touched his, he sucked in a breath, then hurried to sheath himself.

"Take off your shirt." Watching those gorgeous breasts with their pierced nipples bounce as she rode him would most assuredly shove him closer to the edge of orgasm, but he couldn't bring himself to care.

Again, she obeyed without complaint, ridding herself of the tank top and bra in seconds.

"You are the most beautiful woman I've ever seen," he murmured, brushing his fingertips over the ring in her eyebrow, the piercing in the siren's call of her mouth, the hoops in her nipples. A ravenous need gripped him in its greedy claws, but he still traced a path down to her belly and circled the twinkling jewel in her navel. He raised his arms and anchored himself with the headrest once more. "Ride me."

She trembled, and he absorbed the ripple of it. Kneeling above him, she positioned his cock beneath her and slowly, so damn slowly, sank down on him. An almost animalistic wail escaped her, and her hands flattened on his abdomen. A glance down his torso and to the place where they were connected revealed she'd only taken half his length inside her. He waited, giving her time to adjust to a position that would make him seem bigger, thicker. But it cost him. Every quiver of her feminine muscles, every contraction of her slick, smooth walls around him shaved away at his control. Heightened the intensity of the electrical currents sizzling from the base of his neck, down his spine, and to his balls. Even the soles of his feet tingled with awareness of mind-melting pleasure just on the horizon.

"Touch yourself," he instructed, and her gaze rose to meet his. Still trembling like a leaf caught in a fierce wind, she reached between them and hesitantly swept a finger over the clit that peeked out from between her folds. Her cry echoed in the car, her body jerking. Her fingertips—two this time—repeated the caress, and she accepted more of him. Another stroke of those elegant fingers, and over half his cock disappeared inside her. "Keep playing with yourself, baby," he encouraged, and because he couldn't not touch her any longer, he clasped a taut nipple between his finger and thumb. And tugged.

With another of those raw screams, she took all of him. As if those last few inches were a catalyst, she exploded. On a curse, he grabbed her hips, holding her and pumping into her, giving her every bit of the orgasm that seized her. Her sex milked him, drawing on him, pulling him deeper. Her nails bit into him, adding a hint of pain to the pleasure tearing through him.

One stroke. Another. And another. And fuck, there. It ripped him apart, put him back together again, only to do it again. He surged between her thighs like a wild animal, pouring into the condom, and for once, in a brief flash of sanity—or insanity—wished the barrier was gone. That it was just her and him, with nothing separating them.

But then, he wasn't thinking at all.

Just a prisoner of the lust and ecstasy that chained him to her. And he willingly let himself be enslaved.

Even if for a little while.

Chapter Thirteen

Sophia glanced at the clock on her laptop. 4:25. Only thirty-five more minutes to go, and her day would be over. Thirty-five more minutes, and she would head over to the high school to meet Zephirin.

At just the mention of his name, she smiled. A small smile, but one nonetheless. Even though a part of her acknowledged that mooning over a man who believed you were someone else defined the very height of insanity. But...

After sex in his truck a couple of nights ago, her stupid, stubborn, crystal-castles-in-the-sky heart had tried to appropriate her common sense. Insisting maybe their time together didn't need to end when Giovanna returned home. That, yes, he might believe she was someone else, but he did seem to actually like and accept *her*—her quirks, her love of eighties movies, her humor, her piercings and ink. He listened to her, hadn't brushed off her idea about the app. And from the way he couldn't seem to keep his hands off of her and other body parts from inside her, he found her attractive. Maybe, just maybe, he would understand why she'd pretended to be Giovanna all this time.

"That's my one rule, Sophia. Honesty, no lies. Ever."

That had been his rule—his only rule when they'd renegotiated the terms of their arrangement. And the truth besides her being a liar? She wasn't Giovanna. *Could never be*, that insidious voice in her head whispered. The women he usually dated were so far out of Sophia's league, she couldn't even buy tickets to get in the game. Maybe her quirks were acceptable because of *what* he believed her to be—a model, sophisticated, worldly—and not *who*.

Jesus. She was giving herself a headache with the whos, whats, whens, whodidits, and whys.

One thing she knew for certain. Today was Thursday, and Giovanna returned home on Sunday. She had three more days with him. And no way in hell was she squandering them. This time with him would have to last her for a lifetime.

The ringing of her desk phone interrupted her dismal thoughts.

"Thank God," she muttered, picking up the receiver.

"Sophia, I need to see you in my office, please." Brian.

She'd thanked God a little too soon.

Sighing, she trekked down the hall as if her last rites and meal awaited her. Once she stood outside her supervisor's door, she inhaled a deep breath, asked God to increase her patience—and keep the temptation of sharpened pencils away from her—and knocked. After catching his "Come in," she entered.

As always, he sat behind his desk, not bothering to rise when she entered. That shouldn't have irked her, but it did. It probably wouldn't even have bothered her if she hadn't become used to Zephirin rising whenever she left a table or returned to it. Maybe it was a Southern thing, but her boss could learn some manners from her football player.

The football player. *The*. Her football player? Where the hell had that come from?

"Have a seat, Sophia." Brian didn't remove his attention from his computer, clicking on his mouse and typing as she lowered to the chair in front of his desk. After a couple of minutes, he seemed to remember that *he* had invited *her* to his office and switched his regard to her. "I finished reviewing your proposal. Thank you for submitting it so quickly."

"You're welcome." Nerves erupted in her stomach like a flock of mad, hungry geese. She'd been toying with the idea of a virtual dressing room for a little while, and his announcement of a new app had seemed like fate. Her heart sped up in her chest, ready to hear his verdict.

"I was waiting on a couple more proposals, but I've already run this by my supervisor, and yours is the forerunner. This is unofficial, you understand, but the virtual dressing room is going to be chosen as FamFit's new app for development."

Happiness and triumph soared through her, and she clutched the arms of the chair to avoid doing a fist pump in the air. The idea had been a little off the beaten path since the company mainly focused on fitness apps. But a program where customers could enter their measurements and wait while a personal shopper chose exercise and sportswear for them to "try on" from FamFit's webstore had seemed fun. And, for customers like her, it eased the pain of shopping for clothes. She couldn't prevent a grin from widening her lips. "Really?" she asked.

He nodded. "It was excellent work."

"Thank you, Brian," she said, her joy multiplying at the seemingly genuine praise. Maybe she'd misjudged him. "And I won't disappoint you as project manager."

"About that…" He leaned forward, propping his clasped hands on top of the desk. "Like I said, your concept is excellent. But I just don't think you're ready for a position like project manager yet. While you've been here a few years, we need someone with more experience heading this."

Stunned, she stared at him. Heat tinged with disappointment and anger streamed up her chest and throat, pouring into her face. He'd done it to her again. Snatched the rug out from under her and left her sprawled like a trusting idiot.

"When we spoke last week, you assured me that if my app was chosen, I would be project manager," she said past numb lips.

"I said it *could* mean project manager for you. *Could*." He templed his fingers under his chin, contemplating her over the rims of his black glasses. "I'm doing you a favor, Sophia. The position would be time-consuming, requiring longer hours and much more responsibility. You're young, you have a social life, and this would most likely be a burden. I've decided Trevor would be a better fit to head the project. But you can assist him since it was your idea. I'm depending on you for that."

"Trevor is two years older than me and takes off at least two Mondays every month because he's hungover from the weekend," she bit out. Anger. Now that the shock had worn off, anger rushed in like a flood, surging into every part of her, filling her like a dry water bed. She soaked up the rage, frustration, and helplessness like that cracked ground.

This wasn't about experience; this had everything to do with her being a woman and refusing to be one of his sycophants. Out of the three years she'd been working for him, not one woman—including the other one in their department with ten years on the job—had been appointed project manager.

And now, after promising her the job in exchange for her proposal, he'd screwed her. Again.

I quit. The shout quivered on her tongue, begging to be voiced. But reason—and fear—trapped them inside. Yes, she could walk out. And go where? Do what? People who usually walked off a job found it difficult to acquire another position without references. And she didn't need a magic eight ball to reveal that a positive review wouldn't be forthcoming from Brian if she left.

She was as trapped as those words.

And he knew it.

Behind his glasses, he didn't bother hiding the satisfaction or impatience in his gaze. Didn't bother to convince her that she had it all wrong about Trevor. He held a royal flush, and she held a losing, pathetic hand.

"My decision has been made. We'll start Monday. Thank you, Sophia." With that, he turned back to his computer, dismissing her. As unimportant. Inconsequential.

And damn herself to hell for allowing him to make her feel that way.

• • •

Zephirin frowned as Sophia's generic voicemail greeting instructed him to leave a message at the beep…for the fourth time. Unlike the previous three times, he decided to obey.

"Hey, this is Zephirin. Give me a call when you get this. I'm wrapping up here at the camp. If you're running late, we can meet at my place instead of here. Just let me know."

Still frowning, he ended the message, staring down at the phone. Usually, she answered his calls or returned them within minutes. But not today.

Something was wrong. Possibly the same "something" that had been bothering her Tuesday night. The something that had caused the almost desperate glimmer in her eyes. Had incited that crazy but hot sex in his car. And she still hadn't shared the reason.

And yet, in spite of her reticence, lying in his truck,

holding her curved, soft body to his, a peace had stolen over him. A deep satisfaction. Sophia was so damn different from most of the women he'd met since entering the league. Hell, since entering college. Those of his acquaintance, including his ex-girlfriend, saw football players as a ticket or free ride to a wealthy lifestyle. Or a jump off to their own career aspirations.

But Sophia, with her often blunt honesty, sensitivity, and vulnerability, cast all those women in a dark shadow. She was...refreshing. A word he wouldn't have believed he could call anyone in his often jaded world.

Doubt crept into his head, the stealthy intruder issuing warnings. And he couldn't eject them.

He knew better than to paint every woman with the same Shalene-tinted brush—he'd been raised by a selfless, sacrificing, good woman. She'd set an example for him. So he understood that he couldn't blame every female for his ex's mistakes. But Shalene was the yardstick by which he measured the rest. She'd taught him what to be aware of. Missed phone calls were just that—missed phone calls. But the last time he'd trusted in a woman, she'd cleverly hidden her true colors. And though he and Sophia had agreed that their...arrangement was temporary, she very well could play him for a fool.

God. He stuffed his cell in the pocket of his shorts and strode back toward the parking lot where the last bus carrying the kids had left twenty minutes earlier. Sophia should've been at the high school a half hour ago, at five-thirty as they'd discussed. He'd wait another fifteen minutes before leaving.

Shit.

He shoved the bar on the heavy door and stepped out into the evening air and, except for a few remaining vehicles, empty parking lot. Why did it feel like his time with her was ticking away? Starting Monday, he would be attending a mandatory three-day mini-camp that would start early in the morning and last until about seven in the evening, which meant their time together would be limited. And maybe that was for the best. She was everything he didn't—shouldn't—want in a long-term partner. His dream was of a woman outside of this business. A woman who wouldn't see him as either competition or a meal ticket, an opportunity. Plus, he'd promised himself he'd avoid getting wrapped up in a woman while he still held on to his professional career. Because as he'd seen with Shalene, when things went south with a relationship, his ability to focus on the game did, too.

And yet, he couldn't deny that the part of him that was obviously a glutton for punishment had started considering that maybe, just maybe, Sophia was different. That it didn't have to be that way with her...

"Problem?" Shalene appeared next to him, a bag slung over her shoulder, car keys dangling from her fingers. Though she'd attended every day of the camp including today, she still appeared as fresh as she had that morning. Not a strand escaped her high ponytail; the makeup on her smooth cocoa skin was flawless. The purple romper that revealed the long length of her slender legs remained unwrinkled. His ex-girlfriend was as beautiful as she'd been when she'd reentered his life five years ago. And when he'd seen her on the other side of a conference table in his lawyer's office a year and a half ago.

Any man could be forgiven for losing his head over her, for being blind to the things going on.

Any man but him.

"No." He surveyed the lot and the direction of the entrance where Sophia's car would have to travel. No sign of her. The worry wiggling in his gut didn't ease. Attempting to push it aside for the moment, he glanced down at Shalene. "Thank you for all of your help this week. It wouldn't have gone nearly as smoothly without you."

"Of course," she said. "You know this is my passion. It'll never bring Ryan back but…" She trailed off at the mention of her brother's name, then shook her head. "But I love working with the foundation, the boys…and you," she murmured. Shoulders straightening, she tilted her chin up. "I've never said it before, but thank you for letting me continue to work here. After everything that happened…" Again she shook her head. "You would've had every right to ban me from having anything to do with the foundation and fire me. Thank you for giving me another chance."

Surprised, he arched an eyebrow. He could count on one hand the number of times Shalene had apologized for anything. The cynical part of him contended that this overture must hide ulterior motives. He hated that thanks to his experiences with her, seeking someone's angle or motivation had become normal to him.

"You helped me establish it. And I, more than anyone, understand what the cause means to you. I get how important the work is to you, and no matter what happened between us, I wouldn't take that away from you."

"Yes, it is important to me," she agreed, shifting closer to him. Placing a hand on his chest, she tilted her head back, and her eyes darkened with emotion. An emotion he'd long since ceased to reciprocate. "But so are you. You're the other reason I'm glad to still be here. The reason I work so hard to make each event, like the camp, a success."

"Shalene," he warned, covering her hand with his and removing it. But she only circled his arm with the other.

"I'm sorry for hurting you, Zeph. For…for everything. I told myself to give you space, to not pressure you. But I miss you so much. Not only did I lose the man I love, but I lost my best friend. I want him back. I want *us* back. We have too much history together to just let it end like this."

The bitterness and anger he tried to control around her bubbled to the surface. "Leave it alone, Shalene," he warned.

"When are you going to forgive me?" she whispered, her hurt unmistakable.

There was once a time when he would've caved, given her the words just to avoid hurting her feelings. But he couldn't. Ordinarily, he could've buried the hurt and the rage under a blanket of ice. Not today. Not with her reminding him of their *history.*

"Let it end like what? With all the lies you told me? With a call from my bank asking if I'd authorized the thousands of dollars you'd stolen from my account? Or end in a lawyer's office where I found out that the son I thought we'd had together wasn't mine?" he growled, all the disillusion, grief, and agony of that day pouring into him like a flood. "*Shit,*" he ground out, turning away from her, scrubbing a hand over his head. "This is why you should've left it alone. I don't want to go into this. Everything we had to say to each other— anything that needed to be said—was done over a year ago. This is pointless."

It wouldn't erase the joy of watching a baby he'd believed was his being born, of holding him. And it damn sure wouldn't expunge the agony of discovering he wasn't his. It'd been like a death. No words or apology could wipe that away.

"No, not pointless," she argued, shaking her head. She reached out, grasped a hand in hers. Clenching his jaw, he stilled the impulse to jerk free. Whatever their past, he didn't want to harm her physically. "Because if you're still angry with me, it means you have feelings for me. I'm holding on to that."

"Shalene, I can't—"

"I'm sorry. I didn't mean to interrupt." The soft voice might as well as have been blared over a megaphone.

He broke free of Shalene's hold and turned to face

Sophia. For once, her expression didn't reveal her thoughts. She glanced from him to Shalene, then returned her regard to him. Still no hint of emotion. Irritation rolled up inside him, but he almost immediately smothered it. What? Did he want her to go Jerry Springer on his ex? Stake a claim?

Maybe. The sly insinuation slid through his mind before he could bar it.

"I'll wait for you to finish up here," Sophia said, already pivoting to return to the car he hadn't heard pull up.

"No, wait." He reached out, grasped her upper arm and prevented her from taking another step away from him. "Shalene and I were finished."

The other woman hesitated, but then after a long moment, nodded and walked away.

"I could've waited by the car," Sophia said, glancing after his ex. "Whatever you were discussing looked important."

An explanation hovered on the tip of his tongue, but he swallowed it. Talking about Shalene, the hell she put him through, the loss of a son that hadn't been his to begin with... The thought of reliving it tightened his gut into knots, as did the idea of laying his shit out there so she could see how much of a fool he'd been. To this day, he'd only shared all the details with Dom and Ronin.

Instead, he shifted forward, not stopping until her back met the door, the need to distract her—distract himself—a razor-sharp, desperate impulse. He flattened his palms on either side of her head, leaning down until their mouths hovered a bare inch apart. Inhaling, he could already taste her kiss on each breath she released.

"You have a real issue with crowding me," she muttered, her face losing that damn mannequin expression for a scowl. The vise grip on his chest loosened a fraction. "Some would call it intimidation."

"Then some wouldn't know how it felt to have all your

pretty curves pressed against their body. Or know what it is to feel your mouth part under theirs. Or to have your scent in their nose, on their skin. If they did, then this would be their favorite position, too."

Her eyes widened, then became hooded, arousal entering them. Her fingers slipped under the hem of his T-shirt, hooking into the waistband of his shorts, brushing him. That small skin-to-skin contact had his stomach contracting, his cock hardening.

"I know you're trying to sidetrack me," she murmured. Her lips twisted into a caricature of a smile. "But you don't have to tell me about what I walked up on if you don't want to. We have an arrangement, remember? Just sex. Not inquiries into our personal lives."

She was right. They were temporary; fuck buddies with an expiration date. No promises, no expectations. But, *damn*. Though she tried to conceal it from him behind nonchalance, he could spy the hurt in her eyes, in her voice. And yeah, the thought of going into the crap that was his past didn't appeal to him, but the bruises in her gaze punched a hole in his gut.

Yeah, it was too late. Somehow, someway, in spite of every warning his mind had blared, it'd become *personal*.

"She's my ex-girlfriend," he ground out. "Though we've been broken up for a while now, she still works with the foundation."

"She still wants you," she stated just as softly.

"Yes." Denying it would be stupid. Sophia was smart and had eyes.

They stared at each other, the Thursday evening traffic bypassing the school drowning under the weight of the silence between them. Slowly, he eliminated the distance separating their mouths and claimed her. The metal of her ring rubbed against his lip, and he flicked his tongue over the jewelry before grazing her sensual flesh with his teeth. That familiar and damn sexy whimper escaped her, and yeah, he needed another one. He swept inside her mouth, devouring, feasting, his patience incinerated by the hunger that flared to life every time he touched her.

He thrust a hand into her sensual riot of curls and waves, holding her steady for every lick, suck, and taste. No passenger in this passionate ride, she gave as good as she got, meeting him plunge for plunge, stroke for stroke, demand for demand.

By the time he lifted his head, they both shuddered against each other, and his dick desired nothing more than to be buried so deep inside her she would feel him when he was no longer there. The thought of no longer being there— of no longer being able to inhale her sweet scent, listen to her weirdly hot snark, of curling his body around hers in the night—caused his heart to pound a little harder, tightened his gut until it complained as if he'd done a hundred sit-ups. He drowned out the ache and the dangerously sentimental thought with another deep, claiming kiss.

"Now your turn. Tell me what's wrong," he said, tearing his mouth away from hers. He didn't bother asking her *if* something bothered her. He could see it in her eyes, the shadows that darkened them. And he sensed it didn't have to do with his ex-girlfriend. "Let me fix it for you."

She didn't deny his assertion. Instead, a small, almost apologetic smile tilted a corner of her mouth. "You want to slay my dragons?" she murmured.

"If you'll let me."

Her gaze dropped away from his, and though she didn't physically move, a distance seemed to insert itself between them. He hated it. Wanted to ram his body against it, tackle it to the ground.

"Come home with me." A command. A plea that came out of him before he'd consciously given it permission. But once it was out there, he didn't take it back. After the conversation with Shalene—after the raw, still sore emotions she'd dredged to the surface—he needed to find forgetfulness in Sophia's body. He didn't care how she interpreted it, just as long as she said yes.

Her lashes lifted, and she subjected him to a scrutiny that seemed to search him for an answer to a question he didn't know had been asked.

But finally, she nodded. Exhaled a breath. "Okay."

Chapter Fourteen

"Will you tell me about her?" Sophia whispered the question against the bare skin of Zephirin's chest. More like hid her face against him. She sounded like a jealous girlfriend inquiring about the past ones. God knows she'd felt like one when she'd walked up on the two of them at the high school parking lot. Which was ludicrous. No-strings-attached sex did not a girlfriend make. As long as she kept that reminder at the forefront of her brain, then when this arrangement between them ended, the hurt would be minimal.

And she wouldn't go around in danger of snatching up handsy women who dared touch Zephirin in front of her.

She swallowed a sigh. Yeah, that didn't sound jealous. At. All.

Oh well. In for a penny 'n' all that. And damn it, she really wanted to know. "Your conversation seemed really intense. Did she hurt you badly?"

Beneath her, Zephirin's body stiffened, and for a moment, she didn't think he would answer. Would push her away. When he rolled out from under her and sat on the side of the bed, a boulder-size lump settled in the pit of her stomach. Like she'd mentioned earlier, their relationship had boundaries. And obviously, she'd crossed one.

"Here." He handed her the T-shirt she'd stripped off him earlier and swept up his shorts. As he stepped into them, she froze, studying his perfect form. Strong back with muscles that danced with each movement under taut skin. A tapered waist. Firm, gorgeous ass. Powerful thighs. The man was stunning in his masculine beauty.

He glanced over one of those wide shoulders, an eyebrow arched. Blushing, she fumbled into his shirt. Scrambling off the mattress, she stood, and the material hit her at the knees. His earthy scent enveloped her, and she barely smothered the urge to bring the cotton up to her nose and inhale him.

Enfolding her hand in his, he led her from the dimly lit bedroom to the shadowed living room. He left her on the couch, and she curled her legs under her. Light softened the dark as he clicked on a lamp, his footsteps heading in the direction of the kitchen. A short while later, he returned to her, a glass of red wine in each hand.

"This is going to require alcohol?" she teased, accepting the glass, although her stomach knotted with nerves. She could count on one hand the number of times she'd seen Zephirin drink. That he needed one to discuss his ex-girlfriend didn't bode well.

He sank down next to her, and she resented the wedge of space he left between them. Elbows propped on his thighs, he stared straight ahead at the gorgeous view of Seattle at night, his fingers loosely cradling his glass. The dime around his neck swung forward, and she curled her fingers into her palm, quelling the urge to stroke its cool surface and the taut skin beneath it.

"Shalene and I grew up in the same neighborhood, but we didn't really become close until high school. We started dating in my junior year, her sophomore. I guess you could say we were in love—as in love as teenagers can be. She was beautiful, sweet, the smartest girl in the school, and had one hell of a voice. She actually auditioned for *American Idol* her junior year of high school but had to drop out. She found out she was pregnant."

He went silent, a muscle ticking along his strong jaw, his fingers tightening around the glass in his hand. Sophia's heart pounded in her chest. God. If she'd known her question would take him back to an obviously troubled time in his past, she would've minded her own business.

"I'd just been accepted to LSU, but I was prepared to turn it down, get a job, and take care of my responsibilities. But then she miscarried, and I'm not going to lie. I-I..." The muscle in his jaw ticked harder. "A part of me was relieved. I wasn't ready to be a father. To let go of my scholarship and the chance to play football for the university I'd wanted to attend since I was a kid. I would have, but suddenly I didn't have to. We stayed together, but when I left for college, we decided to break up. She had her senior year of high school to finish, and I wanted to start the next phase in my life fresh, without any obligations to anyone but my education and football."

He lifted the glass, sipped, and still kept his gaze fixed on the dark waters of Elliott Bay. Although Sophia doubted he really saw anything; he seemed steeped in the past. A past she'd dredged up.

"After I was drafted to the Warriors, I returned home for a visit with family and saw Shalene again. Of course I'd thought of her in the four years I'd been in college, but seeing her again was almost like the first time back in high school. The feelings rushed back in, and when I left for Seattle a couple of months later, she came with me."

Pinpricks of jealousy stung Sophia over the dizzying fall into love he glossed over but must have felt to move so fast with his high school sweetheart. Sophia and Zephirin had known each other for a short time, but she would've never associated "impulsive" with him. That he'd been so with Shalene only betrayed the depth of his feelings for the other woman. The pinpricks transformed into daggers, and the nicks into cuts. No man had ever loved her so passionately, and she had never experienced that kind of emotion either. Hadn't realized she wanted to until she heard Zephirin talk about him and his beautiful ex-girlfriend.

"For the first two years, we had the perfect relationship," he continued. "I bought us a house, we settled down, formed a life here. She even helped me establish the foundation. I thought we were happy. I thought..." His voice trailed off, and a small hard-edged chuckle escaped him. "Admitting being made a fool of isn't easy."

He surged to his feet, setting the wine on a nearby glass end table. Scrubbing his hands over his closely-shaven head, he paced to the window. Remaining on the couch, Sophia stared at the rigid, uncompromising line of his shoulders, the tautness of his back.

"At first, I didn't notice anything out of the ordinary. For nine months out of the year, football dominates my life, so when she decided to try and pursue a singing career, I supported it. And truthfully, I harbored some guilt regarding it. She'd had to abandon the *American Idol* audition because of the pregnancy. Even after we lost the baby, the opportunity had passed, that particular door closed. But I'd gone on to pursue my dream of playing ball and achieved it. I was partly responsible for her missing out on hers, so I tried to help her emotionally and financially. But she couldn't break through. And with every disappointment, it seemed she became more...desperate for fame, for acknowledgment. She even signed on to do one of those reality TV shows about wives and girlfriends of athletes, promising them I would film. I refused, and the producers eventually dropped her from the show because of it. I think that's when her resentment really started to grow. When she decided to go after what she wanted by any means necessary, not caring who she hurt in the process. When the lies started."

Lies. It echoed in her soul, the loud clang of it an indictment only she could hear and feel. The nerves in her stomach twisted into an almost painful coil.

"Money started disappearing from our joint accounts. Thousands of dollars. She started going MIA for periods of time. Rumors would crop up about her being in one place when she'd told me she had plans to be in another. We stopped talking—or rather she stopped talking to me."

"She was cheating," Sophia breathed, speaking for the first time since he'd started his recount. Disbelief rocked through her. How could anyone want someone else when they had the heart and body of this man?

Zephirin turned around, a corner of his mouth lifted in a humorless smile. "If only it was that simple. Maybe if she had only been screwing another man, spending money on him, it would've been easier, more understandable to eventually accept. The truth is much harder to swallow. Because it means at some point, I had my head so far up my ass, I missed when she became so bitter toward me that stealing my career and my reputation was a means to justify an end."

He retraced his steps across the room and, picking up the wineglass, drained it.

"My agent brought an endorsement opportunity to me that I wasn't too sold on. But after discussing it with Shalene on one of the few times we actually communicated, I decided to do it. Weeks later, Ronin brought certain rumors to my attention. Rumors about me insisting on and receiving kickbacks when signing endorsement deals. I called the most recent company I'd signed on with, and discovered that I had apparently insisted that in order to be the face of their sports drink, my girlfriend had to sing the jingle on all three commercials they planned on filming."

Sophia shook her head, confused. "I don't understand. You—"

"Didn't know a thing about it. That little detail had been added by my agent as payment to Shalene for convincing me to sign the contract."

Shock and disgust gripped her. As did disbelief. "She sold you out."

He snorted, sinking to the couch cushion. "Pimped me out would be a more accurate description. And not for the first time. I confronted my agent, and he confessed the truth. Shalene was his ace in the hole...or his saboteur. She would approach me as the concerned girlfriend, point out the benefits of seeing things my agent's way, and in the end, she would receive a 'bonus.' On the other hand, if nothing was in it for her, she would emphasize why I shouldn't accept. For the athletic clothing line I agreed to endorse, the company agreed to place her in my commercial as well as two more for different products. And all that time, I was the patsy, willfully blinded to their actions. No, not blind. Stupid."

"Trusting. In love," Sophia corrected softly. Daring to move, to touch him, she scooted closer to him and placed a hand on his thigh. "You can't be faulted for that."

"Yes, I can," he argued, but didn't push her hand away. "Trust and love aren't excuses for being a fool. For not taking care of business. For damn near volunteering to be used. That's my fault."

She lightly squeezed the hard muscle beneath her hand. She didn't agree, but no amount of contradicting would change his mind. "I take it you confronted Shalene."

"And she denied it, of course. At first. But when she realized I knew everything, she blamed me for stealing her dreams. Said I owed her. And I stood there wondering if I'd ever truly known her, or if she'd been wearing a mask the entire time we'd been together. If she'd ever been truthful with me, or if we'd always been living a lie." He rubbed a hand over the hair framing his mouth and shadowing his jaw. "She left, and I fired my agent, sold the house I'd bought for us, and moved on. But that wasn't the end of it."

A hollow opened in the pit of her stomach, the dread filling it causing her heart to pound against her rib cage. Not for the first time, she regretted opening this particular door. She had a feeling what he was about to reveal trumped all he'd already shared.

"A week after she moved out, Shalene called and told me she was pregnant. Four months along. I was shocked, of course, but unlike when we were in high school, I welcomed the news. Yeah, me and Shalene were done, and I would've preferred to give a child of mine what I didn't have—parents who loved each other and lived under the same roof. But a baby." He paused, stared straight ahead. "It seemed like I was being offered a second chance at being a father. And this time I could provide for him or her, was in the right place in my life where I could offer a child the world. And be the father my own hadn't been. So, for the child's sake, I put our differences aside and concentrated on co-parenting with Shalene."

Jesus Christ. A baby. He'd never mentioned… That pit in her stomach yawned into a chasm. She forced herself to concentrate on his words instead of the chaotic thoughts and emotions whirling inside her head.

"We had a son. It was the best, the happiest moment of my life. Holding him for the first time, hearing his cry. Until then, I'd believed my purpose in life had been to play ball. But in that moment, it all changed. I knew I'd been born to be a father to my son. Almost immediately, Shalene started playing games, using him to get things out of me, allowing me to see him on her schedule. When she demanded child support, I didn't mind, though. I'd already planned to provide for my son. But I didn't trust her, so I insisted on going through our lawyers to set up the payments and visitations. With child support, I had to take a paternity test, but I didn't care. It was a formality. Only it wasn't."

His voice cracked, and horror filled her. *God, no.* He couldn't mean…

"I entered my attorney's conference room that morning thinking we were going to iron out a visitation plan, and I found out that he wasn't mine. With four words—zero chance of paternity—I discovered she'd cheated on me, and I lost a son."

"Zephirin." It was all she could say. What words could she possibly utter that would ease the pain so obvious in his voice? Her heart hurt for him, cried for him.

"After that, I was so fucked up in the head, my game suffered, my team started losing faith in me, couldn't depend on me to mentally show up. I promised myself then I would never allow anything or anyone else to screw with me like that again. She…stole something from me. My belief in people, my trust, my…" He shook his head. "And I don't think I'll ever get it back."

Mouth as dry as a desert floor, she stared at him, unable to speak. Now she understood why, from the first night they'd met, he'd insisted on honesty. Why he deplored lies. They'd almost shattered his life, almost robbed him of his one security—football. And the person who'd betrayed him had been a woman he'd loved.

"You haven't forgiven her," she finally murmured. *Just like he won't forgive you once he discovers the truth.* The warning whispered through her head, increasing the apprehension and foreboding pressing against her rib cage and leaving no room for air.

The sensual curves of his mouth firmed into a grim line. "It's done and in the past," he stated, voice flat.

That would be a no. The ticking of the clock counting down the time they had left together grew in volume, almost deafening her. Her heart kept time, the rapid pulse beating an urgency through her veins. An urgency she heeded.

Uncaring that only his shirt covered her, she crawled on his lap, straddling him. His semi-hard flesh nestled against her folds, and unbidden, that flame of desire that never really extinguished around him flickered to life. But, for the moment, she ignored it, cupping his face between her palms. The same heat licking at her simmered in his hazel gaze, mingling with the anger, and yes, pain. Though she had no doubt he would deny the pain.

"Do you remember calling me a romantic? You said I watched my eighties movies for the romance. And yeah, you got me there…though I will never admit it again outside of these walls. But there's another reason I've always been drawn to them. It never fails that the good person wins in the end. Nerd, unpopular, misfit, misunderstood, different— doesn't matter. They always triumph, and the assholes get what they had coming. I wish life was like that. But it's not. Most of those bullies who made my life a living hell all those years ago have gone on to have successful careers, families, and seem happy. I should know; I checked on Facebook." And even at work, Brian got away with giving her the shaft.

"Is this a pep talk?" He arched an eyebrow, skepticism filling his voice. But the shadows in his gaze had diminished.

"It is, and I never claimed to be good at them." She glared at him but probably ruined the effect of it by brushing her mouth over his. "What I'm saying is life often sucks. People act like they've lost their damn minds. Those we love and rely on to be our soft landing place snatch the safety net out from under us. Your agent betrayed the trust you'd placed in him. Shalene turned into a…" Stupid bitch. A bitch because she'd wounded Zephirin so deeply. Stupid because she'd had this proud man's heart and had been so cruel, careless, and selfish with it. And all for fleeting things like money and fame. "Anyway, we can't control that, and we damn sure can't go all *Kill Bill* and ensure they get what's coming to them. But what we can control is us. Our spirit, our hearts, our actions, and reactions. We can let the hurt and bitterness pollute us, or we can let it go—let them go—and allow all the shit to teach us, not scar us."

His only reply was the flexing of his fingers at her waist. And the piercing intensity of his scrutiny.

"You"—she grazed his bottom lip with her teeth, soothed the sting with the tip of her tongue—"are beautiful"—a kiss pressed to the top lip—"strong"—another to the corner of his mouth—"honorable"—and another to the opposite corner—"giving"—one more to his chin—"and hot as fuck." At his grunt of laughter, she grinned. "Don't ever change."

Sliding a hand under her shirt, he cupped her breast, toyed with the piercing. Her breath snagged in her lungs, and the smoldering fire inside her flashed into a full-out conflagration. He leaned forward, caught her mouth with his, swallowing her whimper.

And as he rolled, and his big body covered hers on the couch cushions, his mouth closing over her nipple, one thought prevailed before passion erased all logical thought.

She had to tell him the truth.

Even if it meant losing him.

Even if it meant breaking her.

Chapter Fifteen

"I'm feeling all flattered that you tore yourself away from your girl to come work out with me." Dom shot Zephirin a grin as he pushed out of the gym door and into the late Saturday morning sunshine.

Well, sunshine might be a little generous, Zephirin mused, squinting up at the slightly overcast sky. The rain hadn't made an appearance all week long, for which he'd been grateful with the summer camp. But they were due. And like true Seattle weather, when the rain eventually did roll in, it would hang around for a few days as if making up for lost time before blowing back out to sea. Maybe it would continue to hold out for just a while longer. With a mandatory mini-camp next week, his time with Sophia would be a little more limited. He'd planned to take her to Central Cinema that evening. Not only did the movie theater offer full-service dinner, but they showed retro and classic films. Tonight's showing? *The Lost Boys*.

He smiled, imagining her reaction.

"Oh fuck," Dom muttered, heading down East Pike

Street where the Capitol Hill gym was located. The small training center was nowhere near his friend's Kirkland home, but Dom preferred the plain grittiness of the place. Claimed it reminded him of home. "You're smiling for no damn reason. You, of all people. This thing with the model is more far gone than I originally thought."

"What the hell are you talking about now?" Zephirin asked. Dom made it sound like he walked around with a puss on his face. He wasn't that bad...was he? He frowned.

"Last time we talked about Giovanna Cruz, you were denying anything more than a hit-it-and-quit-it existed between the two of you—"

"I never said anything about a hit-it-and-quit-it," Zephirin interrupted. Even when they'd agreed to only a night, he'd never considered her someone to be discarded like a used tissue.

"Oh that's right. You planned on fucking her out of your system. My bad," Dom amended.

Zephirin grimaced. That didn't sound any better now than it had when Ronin had suggested it. And when he'd offered the same arrangement to Sophia.

"Now, you've been spending every evening with her. She's slept at your place where, as far as we know, no woman has ever been invited, and you're just *smiling*." His friend added a mock shudder. "What the hell, man?"

"We're..." His frown deepened.

"Hanging? Smashing? Screwing like demented rabbits?" his friend supplied.

"Are you serious?" Zephirin shook his head, splaying his hands wide, palms up. "Hell, I don't know what we're doing or what we are."

"Hmm."

"Hmm?" Zephirin repeated with a snort. "Is that your Iyanla Vanzant imitation? Needs work."

"Is this you trying to dodge the question?" Dom persisted.

"Was there a question?"

Dom studied him, eyes narrowed. "It's like that, huh?" he asked after a long moment. "So when did it go from casual fucking to 'I don't know what we're doing'?"

"I..." The denial hovered on his tongue, but he couldn't utter it.

Because he couldn't refute Dom's claim that this *thing* between him and Sophia—*arrangement* no longer seemed like an appropriate term—had become more. He also couldn't pinpoint the moment when it had changed.

Didn't want to admit that acknowledging it scared the shit out of him.

This was supposed to be uncomplicated, straightforward lust and sex. A walk-away-no-regrets-or-backward-glances agreement. The last time he was involved with a woman, he hadn't walked away...he'd crawled. And the thought of being that vulnerable, in pain, and out of control again had icy slivers of unease sliding through him.

And then he still couldn't shake the feeling that Sophia harbored secrets. Or maybe secrets was too strong a word. But she held something back; she'd never explained what had been bothering her that night in the car. And he'd never asked her about where she'd been Thursday night when she'd been late to show up at the high school.

To another man, these things wouldn't rise to the level of questionable. But he'd learned the hard way to pay attention to that instinct insisting something was not quite right.

"Hey, isn't that your girl?" Dom's question snapped him out of his thoughts. He paused next to the hood of his truck, but his attention was fixed across the busy street.

Zephirin scanned the buildings. A consignment shop, a skate store, a closed nightclub, and—there. In front of the deli restaurant a couple stood close to each other. The guy, several inches taller than the woman, lowered his head to hers and kissed her brow. She wrapped her arms around his waist, cuddling against him. When she pressed her cheek to his chest, Zephirin had a clear view of her face.

Sophia.

With another man.

When she'd told Zephirin she had to work for a few hours that morning.

A cold numbness spread through his body, paralyzing him so all he could do was watch as she tilted her head back and smiled widely up at the man who returned her grin. They appeared close, familiar. Intimate.

"Zeph," Dom said, as anger started to burn through the paralysis. "He could be anyone—"

"Let's go," he bit out.

A scowl darkened Dom's face, but he remotely released the locks on the vehicle and stalked around the front. Zephirin jerked open the passenger door and slid inside.

There was always an explanation. Always an excuse.

But he didn't know if there was anything left in him to believe them.

• • •

Sophia yanked the front door to her town home open and grinned at the person standing on the other side of the threshold.

Giovanna returned the smile even as she spoke into the cell phone pressed to her ear. "Yes, Mama. I will." Pause. Eye roll. "I just got to Fi's house, so I'll call you back." Another pause and nod even though their mother obviously couldn't see the gesture. "I will. Okay. Love you." Lowering the phone with an exaggerated grimace, she laughed and threw her arms around Sophia. She returned the hug, squeezing her twin.

God, she'd missed her. Usually, they talked at least twice a day and saw each other three to four times a week. With Giovanna being out of the country, Sophia hadn't been able to catch up with her best friend and closest confidante, and it'd been hell. Especially given the recent turn of events.

Sex-only arrangement with Zephirin.

Her job.

Falling for Zephirin.

Just the terrifying thought creeping through her mind had Sophia holding Giovanna tighter. And if there was a hint of desperation in the embrace, well... She'd never been able to hide anything from her other half.

"*Hola, chica*," Giovanna greeted. "I need to leave the country more often so you can appreciate me when I'm here," she joked. "But can I come in at least?"

"Oh shut up," Sophia muttered, releasing her and, grabbing her hand, dragged her inside off the porch.

At one time, Giovanna had crashed in the two-bedroom, two-bath apartment before finding her own place. So when her sister headed straight for the kitchen and refrigerator, it was with the movements of someone who was comfortable and at home. Moments later, Giovanna gracefully dropped onto the couch, iced tea in hand.

"Mama said she loves you, and she's expecting you at dinner on Sunday. She's cooking *arroz con pollo*."

Horror slid through Sophia. "*No*," she gasped.

"Yes." Giovanna shook her head. "I blame Papa for this. He should've told his wife a long time ago that her chicken and rice tastes like cafeteria mystery meat. Oh." A wicked smile curved her mouth. "She's also invited Red."

"Which Red? There are a few Reds." True. In their neighborhood, it was typical to refer to someone by their physical characteristics, and there were several gingers. Almost no one knew their real names; honestly, as far as most people were concerned, the nicknames *were* their real names. Skinny chick. Fat guy. Little kid with the big nose. That's how the neighborhood identified them. Yep, charming.

"*Flacito rojo.*" Skinny Red, shortened to just Red in English. "Marcella's son," Giovanna supplied.

Sophia flipped through her mental Rolodex and finally settled on an image of a stout, bull-necked man with brick-red hair and ruddy skin. In his case, the "skinny" was definitely ironic.

"No." Sophia groaned, covering her face. "Please tell me, not him. He has the personality of a potato. For the love of all that's holy, why?"

Giovanna shrugged, the glass she lifted for a sip not hiding her shit-eating grin. "She thinks you two would make a cute couple. He has a job, comes from a good family, and would take care of you. Her words, not mine."

"I think I'm coming down with the bird flu. Or mad cow disease," Sophia complained.

"As if that's going to work." Giovanna snickered.

Relegating the upcoming torture of Sunday dinner to the side, Sophia shook her head and smiled at her sister. "I thought you were coming home tomorrow," she said, curling up in the chair across from the couch.

Mirroring Sophia's position, Giovanna tucked her feet under her thighs. "I was able to catch an earlier flight." She eyed Sophia over the rim of her glass. "I tried calling you this morning to see if you wanted to catch breakfast, but you didn't answer. So I took Raymond instead. And believe me, he was delighted with a free meal."

Sophia didn't doubt it. Giovanna had met the other man through their modeling agency. But last year, he'd semi-retired from fashion and had opened a gay nightclub in Capitol Hill. Though the club had proved to be a popular hot spot, his finances were still touch-and-go, so when the opportunity for free anything came up, he snatched it.

"Sorry. I would've loved to hang with you two, but I had to go to work for a few hours," Sophia explained.

"On a Saturday?" Her sister frowned. "That's unusual."

Sophia sighed, resting her head on the back of the chair. "Brian called a meeting to discuss an upcoming project." All the details about the app proposal spilled from her, including the promise of project manager to the denial of the position, as well as her anger and hurt over the decision.

When she finished, Giovanna set her tea on the coffee table in front of the couch and slowly unfolded her legs. Then, in a burst of furious motion, she shot to her feet and paced from the sofa to the window and back, her long legs chewing up the compact space. Her sundress tangled around her legs, but it didn't impede her enraged stride.

"*Hijo de puta! Pendejo! Me cago en su madre,*" Giovanna hissed, fists clenched at her sides.

Sophia blinked. Wow. *Son of a whore. Goat pube. I shit on his mother.* Damn. Giovanna was *mad.*

"Umm…you okay?" Sophia asked.

"Why aren't you upset?" Giovanna whirled on her, fists planted on her hips. "Why aren't you down at that office ripping him a new one? I'll hold him down while you kick that little shit in the balls to show him where they're at."

"One, because vigilantism is a punishable offense. And 'Your Honor, he's a misogynistic, lying asshole' isn't a defense."

"You make jokes, and meanwhile, Brian is shafting you left and right. This isn't the first time, and as long as you bend over and take it, it won't be the last," her twin raged.

Suddenly tired, Sophia rubbed her forehead where a dull ache had started pulsing. "You think I don't know that? You think I didn't sit there this morning feeling like a powerless, spineless doormat while I explained to Trevor how the app

I created would work? Explained to the project manager—
the job that had been promised to me—how to do his job
while all along Brian sat there, a smug smile on his face? You
don't think I wanted to shout at the unfairness, at the utter
helplessness I felt? But what can I do? Quit?"

"Yes."

Sophia's laughter scraped a throat sore from a morning
of holding in curses and screams. Of course that would be
her twin's response. Giovanna had always been the bolder
of the two. The little girl from South Park who'd dreamed
of becoming one of the few supermodels of Puerto Rican
descent hadn't let anything stand in her way. If someone had
built a wall, Giovanna wouldn't bother going around it; she
charged right through, smashing it down and daring anyone
to say a word. Sophia had always admired that about her
twin, but she herself lacked that vivaciousness, that spirit.
That courage.

"You make it sound so simple," Sophia said, shaking her
head.

"It is." Giovanna crossed the floor and knelt down in front
of Sophia's chair, clasping her hands in hers. "You've always
underestimated yourself. Your brilliance, your worth. Yeah,
you've come a long way since we were young, but you still
don't see. FamFit courted *you* while you were still in college.
They came after *you*. As did other companies. Not because
they were hard up for developers and computer analysts. But
because you are scary smart, creative, and innovative. I've
always been in awe of your brain, how you think. Stop limiting
yourself. Stop allowing other people to put you inside this
confined, suffocating box and tell you what you're capable of.
When you let people define your world, it will always be too
small for you."

"I'm not you," Sophia whispered, the ache in her voice
a reflection of the hurt, frustration, and deferred hope that

welled in her chest.

"No, you're not," her sister agreed. "You're you. You, who didn't let ignorant bullies destroy you. You, who teachers asked to assist in teaching computer classes her junior year of high school. You, who created your first program in college. You, who has earned FamFit millions of dollars with the apps you've developed in the short time you've been there. You, who once imagined writing your own video game and interactive programs to entertain and teach children. You, who has the balls to do it if you would only take a risk."

Giovanna's words pierced her heart and tunneled through bone and tissue to her soul. To the place where she'd locked away childhood dreams in the favor of a practical, real life with benefits, a regular salary, and 401k. Only one other time had the rusty lock on that sealed door cracked open. When she'd been sitting on a set of high school bleachers watching teen boys play football at a summer camp. When the idea for the interactive app for Zephirin's foundation bloomed in her mind. When she'd shared her idea with him, and he hadn't waved it aside but embraced it, loved it.

If you would only take a risk.

Her sister's words reverberated in her head, playing on a relentless, never-ending loop. Giovanna was wrong; Sophia had taken a risk. Pretending to be her on the photo shoot. Going home with Zephirin that night. Agreeing to spend more time with him.

Falling in love with him.

Sophia briefly squeezed her eyes shut, the now familiar edges of panic and sadness lodging in her heart like a pebble in a shoe. That was her biggest gamble to date. Falling in love with a famous football player who believed she was a successful, gorgeous model who also happened to be her twin sister. Yeah, she'd been taking risks lately, and she didn't know if she had it in her for one more.

"Just think about it, okay?" Giving her hand one last squeeze, Giovanna rose and returned to the couch, reclaiming her perch on the cushions. "We're going out to celebrate my glorious conquering of Milan and my triumphant return home. So go find your sexiest outfit..." She tapped her bottom lip with a fingertip. "Never mind. Scratch that. I'll find something for you at my place. Raymond is giving us VIP treatment at his club tonight."

"I...can't." Her sister's gaze narrowed, and Sophia wished she could slink away and avoid it. *Shit's about to hit the fan.* "I kind of...have plans."

"You can't break them?" Giovanna asked, a speculative gleam entering her eyes.

She could, but she didn't want to. Tonight was her last night with Zephirin. Tonight she would tell him the truth. Tonight she would find out if he hated her or not.

"No, I can't. Sorry."

"Wait a second. Is this a date? Who—" Giovanna sucked in a breath, her eyes widening. "Please," she whispered. "Please tell me you aren't still seeing Zephirin Black."

"Giovanna..." Sophia said.

"Fi, what are you doing?" she whispered, shaking her head. "I thought you ended it. You said it was a one-night thing. Does he know that I'm you? Or you're me? God, this is so confusing," she muttered, pinching the bridge of her nose.

"I don't know. And no, to both versions." Propping her elbows on the chair arms, Sophia covered her face with her hands as if she could hide from her sister's questions and censure. "I think I'm in love with him." The confession came out muffled, but it was unmistakable. As was the crush of anxiety and fear.

Silence met her outburst. And when she inched down her hands away from her face, the concern and sympathy on her sister's face almost made her hide behind them again.

"Please don't look at me like that," Sophia pleaded with a small huff of breath. "I already know how hopeless and pathetic I am."

"What are you going to do?" Giovanna asked softly. "And how can I help?"

Love for her sister poured through Sophia and uncapped the well of tears she'd been holding back. "I have to tell him the truth. I know it might hurt your career, Vanna—"

"Forget that," she interrupted with a slice of her hand through the air. "I'll handle it. I'm more worried about you. What if..." She paused. "What if he doesn't forgive you?"

Sophia swallowed past the lump blocking her windpipe. A lump comprised of guilt, apprehension, and dread. Zephirin rejecting her and walking away without a backward glance presented a very real possibility. But she couldn't keep the truth from him any longer. Not after what he'd revealed to her two nights earlier about Shalene. Not if she wanted to find out if there was even the most remote chance they could turn this temporary deal into more.

Not if she loved him.

"I have to take that chance," she said to Giovanna's question. "Continuing to lie to him isn't an option any longer. I..." She lifted a shoulder in a half shrug.

Thursday night, she'd glimpsed something in his eagle eyes. Something that had given her hope that maybe, just maybe there could be a "them." And now she placed everything on that sliver of hope.

"Well." Giovanna rose from the couch, clapping her hands together once. "What time are you supposed to see him?"

"I'm meeting him at his place at six."

"It's one o'clock now. My offer for a sexy outfit still stands. If you're determined to spill the beans tonight, then we need to squeeze you into the skimpiest, tightest dress possible.

T&A does wonders for forgiveness." Giovanna studied her. "Makeup will help, too."

In spite of the nerves playing kick ball with her organs, Sophia laughed. "Do I have a choice?"

"Nope. Let's go. My closet awaits."

"Fine," Sophia grumbled, standing and heading for her bedroom to grab her shoes and bag. "But I'm not wearing anything tight or skimpy."

Giovanna chuckled, following her. "Oh, it's so cute that you really believe that."

Chapter Sixteen

Zephirin stared at Sophia's door, a litany of curses streaming through his head.

This was fucking stupid.

He was acting like a jealous asshole.

Shit.

He and Sophia had agreed to meet for dinner at his place at six o'clock. This could've waited until then. Like Dom had mentioned, there was probably a reasonable explanation regarding the guy she'd been with when she'd told Zephirin she would be at work.

She started going MIA for periods of time. Rumors would crop up about her being in one place when she'd told me she had plans to be in another.

His words to Sophia about the end of his relationship with his ex-girlfriend haunted him. The similarities...

This is bullshit, he argued with himself. The truth of the matter was, Sophia really didn't owe him an explanation. The two of them weren't in an exclusive relationship—hell, they weren't even in a relationship. Sex with an end date. That's what they had. All they'd agreed to.

He'd repeated that logic to himself the entire drive to her Belltown building. Had again reminded himself of it as he climbed the steps to her apartment and stood in front of it a whole hour and a half before their date.

And yet, here he remained, knocking on her door to do what, exactly? Demand to know who the hell the guy had been? Fuck it. Yeah, he wanted to know. Because just the mental image of another man skimming his hands over those dangerous curves and smooth skin had his own fingers itching to tear someone apart. Preferably the pretty boy he'd seen her with.

As he lifted his arm to knock again, he caught voices behind the door. Seconds later, it opened, and he stared into her beautiful face. The face that only hours ago had been wrapped in a smile when it'd been upturned for another man, as if waiting for a kiss.

"Sophia," he said. But then stopped. Frowned. Something was…off. Different. Several more moments passed where she gaped at him, and it struck him. No piercings in her bottom lip and eyebrow. The bright blue tips had been dyed the same brown as the rest of her hair. In the body-hugging sundress, she appeared more like the model he'd met a year ago than the woman who had become his obsession in the last few days.

"Zephirin," she whispered. "Uh, what are you doing here?"

Good question. "I needed to talk to you. Can I come in?"

"Umm…" She tossed a nervous glance over her shoulder, and a vise grip clapped around his rib cage, tightening, constricting until he wouldn't have been surprised to hear a bone snap. A week ago, she hadn't hesitated to invite him into her home. Why now? Was someone there? The guy from the deli? With a sigh, she stepped aside, and he stepped into the apartment. "Listen," she said, closing the door behind him, "this isn't a—"

"Giovanna, this is the only thing in your closet I'm compromising...on..." The voice reached him seconds before another woman strode into view from behind the partition separating the living area from the bedroom.

A woman identical to the one standing in the doorway except for piercings, blue hair, and the blue, green, and yellow tail of a peacock tattoo peeking above the hem of her jeans.

Even though his gaze registered what he saw, disbelief and shock robbed him of speech, thought, the ability to move.

Twins.

Identical twins.

And the one he'd been spending time with, sharing his body and confidences with, had just called the other Giovanna.

"Zephirin," the pierced and inked twin rasped, stumbling forward, a hand outstretched toward him.

Her hesitant movement snapped his paralysis. The numbness didn't slowly melt or ebb away, it splintered, smashed like a shattered windshield on impact. Sprinkling him with shards of memories.

Call me Sophia... Giovanna is the model. Sophia is the woman you described. The woman whose eyes are begging you to fuck her.

I've only been here a short time. I guess 'home' still is my old apartment until I get used to living here.

I'm so not who you think I am.

The clues, the hints, the signs—they'd been there all along. And like with Shalene, he'd chosen to ignore them. Had willingly blinded himself to them. He'd ignored his instinct and had been played.

Again.

"Is your name really Sophia?" he asked, his voice serrated

by disillusionment, smoldering anger, and fucking pain. He'd sworn never to be in this place again. Promised himself he would never be as vulnerable. Yet, she made a liar out of him. Two liars, standing face-to-face.

Guilt tautened her expression as she lowered her arm and wrapped it around her waist. "Yes," she said, her tone thick with, what? Tears? Pain? She could keep both. He wasn't buying either. "Giovanna's my twin sister."

"I guessed that," he drawled, flicking a glance in the other woman's direction before returning his attention to Sophia. *God*. Just saying her name made him cringe. Made him feel like even more of a fool. Had she laughed every time he'd spoken her name? Gotten a kick out of conning him into calling her by her actual name?

"Look, Zephirin," Giovanna said, glancing at her sister. "This is all my fault—"

"Vanna, can you give us a minute?" Sophia directed the question to her twin—the twin he'd believed her to be all this time—but her gaze remained on him.

"Are you sure?" the model murmured. When Sophia nodded, she pinned Zephirin with a hot glare that would've been amusing at another time. But now, at this moment, he couldn't summon up any emotion other than anger and bitterness. "Okay, I'm going for a walk…somewhere. Be back."

With that she left the apartment, leaving just the two of them. No, three of them. Him, her, and the lie. The huge, humiliating lie.

"I'm so sorry, Zephirin," she whispered. "I planned on telling you everything tonight—"

He barked a hard crack of laughter. "Save it. Just tell me, was this some kind of twin joke? You take her place and see if anyone could figure it out? Was this your twisted version of revenge on the football players who bullied you? Hell, I don't even know if that was true," he said, shaking his head.

She paled, reeling back for a moment before straightening. He fisted his fingers by his thighs, calling himself ten different kinds of fool for the involuntary impulse that surged within him—the one that had him taking a step toward her, to touch her, comfort her. God*damn*. A masochistic part of him must enjoy being humiliated.

"*No*," she breathed. Then stronger, "No. All that was true. I swear. And this wasn't revenge or payback. Giovanna had an opportunity to walk in a show in Italy, and she asked me to take her place in the *Sports Unlimited* shoot. It was a one-time deal, something I'd never done before. And you..." She shook her head, her eyes dark with what appeared to be shame, regret. More lies. He couldn't believe anything about her. "You were unexpected. I didn't intend to see you again. I didn't..." Her voice trailed off.

"Didn't what?" he continued, bitterness eating away at him. "Plan to make the conscious decision to lie to me every time you saw me? Let me believe you were someone else? Give me the chance to decide for myself if I wanted to take part in whatever charade you and your sister cooked up?"

"I wanted to tell you. So many times. But I didn't know if you would reveal the truth to *Sports Unlimited* and hurt her career. I couldn't risk that for her. And then...the first time I tried, you told me to let it go. You didn't want to hear it, to make our arrangement any deeper or more complicated than what it was—a temporary fling. Then the more time I spent with you, I became afraid to admit I'd lied. That I continued to lie. Because there came a point when it was less about Giovanna and more about losing you. I wanted to hoard every minute, every second I could with you before I had no choice but to tell you. And I had every intention of doing so, Zephirin. Tonight. I'd intended to confess everything tonight."

"And I should believe you?" He swore under his breath, releasing a low, harsh chuckle. "Hell, I don't *know* you."

"Yes, you do," she objected, shifting forward. "You know about my past, my likes, my dislikes. You know things about me that I have trouble even admitting to myself. You see me. One of the few people who do. No, I'm not a model—"

"Let me guess. You're the sister who's an app developer," he interjected.

She nodded. "Yes. Zephirin, you were unexpected. This surprise gift that wasn't mine, and I was too selfish to give back. And I don't know if I can ever forgive myself for hurting you, but I'm sorry. I'm so sorry."

She took another step, reaching for him. And for a second, he was so desperate for her touch—so desperate to *believe her*—that he almost met her halfway. Almost took that delicate hand in his and dragged her into his arms, against his body. Almost decided to forget the deception, the pain, the disillusionment.

Almost.

Pivoting, he stalked toward the door. He was done. They—whatever they were, whatever they could've been— were done. He couldn't open himself to the kind of agony Shalene had wreaked in his life before. Couldn't risk trusting Sophia only to have her destroy him in a way his ex-girlfriend had tried but hadn't accomplished. But Sophia. She could do it. Easily. The stirrings of that devastation clawed at his chest, and since he couldn't trust himself around her, he couldn't be around her.

"Zephirin," she murmured. He didn't turn around. Couldn't look into that beautiful, deceitful face. "I love you."

"Love me?" he repeated, the words tasting like dirt on his tongue. The pain of hearing the words he hadn't even realized he'd craved until this moment tearing a hole inside him. "Love isn't built on lies. It doesn't purposefully deceive.

I asked you for one thing, Sophia. One. Honesty. If you *loved* me, you would've given that to me."

"And what about you?" she demanded. "You lied, too."

Incredulous, he spun around, facing her. What the hell was she talking about?

"You asked me to share myself with you. The real Sophia. You told me to trust myself with you. Promised you wouldn't reject me." Her voice cracked on the last word, but she continued on. "Here I am, Zephirin. Imperfect. Sometimes not as brave as I should be, but willing to look you in the face and admit it. Willing to lay myself out there, be naked with you. Tell you I love you. But nothing I say, nothing I do will be enough. If you're honest, you would admit you've been waiting for me to fail, to prove you right so you could walk away without any risk, any sacrifice."

She notched her chin up, stared into his eyes without flinching.

"Love isn't built on lies? Love isn't built on unforgiveness either. And I never stood a chance. No one will unless you let go of the past and stop holding everyone hostage to the low standard set by a self-centered, spiteful woman who couldn't appreciate your heart when she had it. I'm not her. I could never be her. For one, I don't even have your heart, and I cherish it. Would fight for it. But the one person I can't battle is you."

This time, instead of moving toward him, she stepped backward. Away from him.

"Good-bye, Zephirin."

She didn't wait for him to leave but turned and walked off, disappearing behind the partition and granting him what he'd wanted but now detested.

Leaving him alone.

Chapter Seventeen

Monday mornings sucked on principle, but when your body was riddled with pain, and every breath you took seemed edged with a razor, well, it sucked more than usual.

Dramatic much? Sophia sighed as she stepped into the elevator that would deposit her at her office floor. She wished she were being a drama queen, but God, she hurt. Ever since Saturday afternoon and the confrontation with Zephirin.

Confrontation. Such a benign word to describe the blow-up that had ripped her heart out of her body. Damn, why were all her metaphors so freaking...bloody?

Definitely showed her frame of mind.

Silently, she watched the numbers light up then darken, slowly counting down to her eminent arrival to FamFit and Brian. To the time she would have to paste a smile on her face and act like everything was hunky-dory. To the time she would have to pretend that not only had the man she loved rejected her but that she was perfectly okay with her boss screwing her over.

Yay.

Unbidden, a groan slipped from between her lips. She closed her eyes, grateful that, for once, no one else occupied the elevator. No one else was there to witness the misery and agony that had leveled her for the past two days.

Yes, she'd fucked up. And she'd always known Zephirin would be angry. But a part of her—that stubbornly, foolishly optimistic part that hadn't been stamped out by four years of high school hell—had hoped he would listen to her. Understand the reasons why she'd lied and continued the charade. Forgive her. That part hadn't expected him to be so hard, so…cold.

She shivered, again hearing the freezing whip of his voice when she'd admitted her love for him.

I asked you for one thing, Sophia. One. Honesty. If you loved me, you would've given that to me.

Jesus, that had hurt. A breath shuddered in and out of her lips.

In the time they'd spent together, she'd started to believe she could trust him with the real her. That he wouldn't reject her but would accept her. He'd crushed that hope under his contempt. Crushed it to dust.

The steel doors slid open with a soft hiss. Inhaling, she stepped out, straightening her shoulders, bracing herself for the day. She passed the floor's breakroom, and as she stepped into the space containing the labyrinth of cubicles, she nearly stumbled.

Trevor stood at the end of the hall, joking with two other guys from their department. Stubble dusted his jaw, and his rumpled clothes had probably been the first ones he'd picked up this morning off the floor. It wouldn't be the first time he'd come in wrinkled and slightly hungover after a night of drinking. Yeah, maybe she was being unfair in her judgment, and this morning he just didn't feel like ironing his polo and khakis.

But the fact that he'd been assigned to lead a project that had been her idea wasn't fair either.

Suddenly, Giovanna's words from Saturday swamped her head, echoing over and over.

Stop allowing other people to put you inside this confined, suffocating box and tell you what you're capable of. When you let people define your world, it will always be too small for you.

Her heart lodged in her throat, thudding there. Though she'd emerged from high school, excelled in college, and had gotten a job in a field she loved, she'd still allowed the taunts and opinions of others from so long ago to define her. Dictate her worth. Convince her to settle.

Even with Zephirin, she'd allowed her fears of him not accepting and appreciating the real her keep her from telling him the truth. The other reasons—Giovanna's job, his hatred of lies—they were all valid. But if she were honest with herself, lurking under those excuses was her own lack of confidence. Her own low image of herself.

And she'd allowed that same lack of self-esteem to quiet her at work.

Well, no more.

Striding past Trevor and his crew, she turned left at the corner instead of right toward her desk.

Seconds later, she stopped in front of Brian's office. She didn't give herself a chance to second guess her decision. Not when the sense that this was *right* clamored inside her like the freaking Liberty Bell.

Rapping on his door, she waited until Brian glanced up from his computer and acknowledged her presence.

A slight frown wrinkled his brow. "Good morning, Sophia."

"Hi, Brian. Can I speak to you?"

"Actually, this isn't a good time…"

He trailed off, and ordinarily, she would have taken the hint and left. But not today. "This will only take a few moments."

He sighed and leaned back in his chair. "Fine. But that's all I have. Come in."

Gritting her teeth together against the condescending tone, she entered and closed the door behind her. His eyebrows arched at the action, but she didn't explain until she sat across from him.

"I quit." Well damn. Okay, she hadn't meant to be that blunt. But since she had, she gave a mental shrug. Might as well go with it. "I hate to give you such short notice, and I appreciate the experience and opportunities that FamFit have given me, but I'm resigning. Effective immediately."

He gaped at her, his lips parted, eyes unblinking. For once, his usual patronizing and arrogant expression was replaced by utter shock. Relief and a fierce joy raced through her. A heavy, crippling weight slid off her chest and shoulders. And for the first time in longer than she could remember, she really, really liked herself. Forget that. *Loved* herself.

She fucking *rocked*.

"What—wait. Why..." he stuttered, before snapping his lips closed and visibly gathering himself. He leaned forward, pinning her with a narrowed stare. "What are you talking about? You can't just quit."

"But I did," she countered. And smiled.

"Is this about not receiving the project manager position? I thought we discussed why you weren't ready for that responsibility—"

"No," she interrupted. "You explained, and I let you get away with that ridiculous, bigoted, bullshit reason. We both know you never intended to give me that job. Just as you took credit for my past contributions and never treated me as an equal. I could never figure out if it was because I'm a woman or you just didn't respect me as a person. Right now, it doesn't matter because I no longer care. I don't need your validation of how good I am. The fact that you shafted me three times is affirmation enough."

"That's ridiculous," he snapped, an unbecoming shade of red coloring his cheeks. A vein appeared at his temple, pulsing. "You're too immature to understand—"

"Too immature. Too young. Too inexperienced. And I also have a vagina. All reasons you've used to disrespect and discriminate against me. And would continue to do if I stayed here. Which I'm not." She stood, never breaking eye contact with him. "I'm going to clear my desk out now, before security is called to escort me out. Which I fully expect you to do." Seeing as he was a petty asshole. "I'll email my formal resignation."

"If you think I'll give you a recommendation, you're deluding yourself. No one will hire you after this behavior," he sneered, that careful composure he always seemed to exhibit gone to reveal the spiteful little bastard he'd always been.

If he expected that to intimidate her, put her back in her place, he'd obviously missed the memo. The one she'd just delivered stamped with a bright red Fuck You seal. She leaned forward and flattened her palms on his desk.

"You go right ahead," she said, her voice calm, strong. "You start your little smear campaign against me because I dared to stand up for myself and demanded to be treated with the dignity and respect I deserve. Because the moment you do, I plan to respond with my own story. Of how you said I should just be patient and my time would come, while you took credit for my ideas. Of how I know for a fact I don't get paid as much as the newest male hire. Of how FamFit prides itself on equal opportunity but really allows misogynistic, little men to get away with promoting other men in their company while expecting women to toe the line and wait their turn for recognition and the opportunities men are simply afforded because they have dicks. As a matter of fact, I'm begging you to try it. You think you can shut me up just because I've allowed you to do it for the last three years? I have breaking news for you, Brian. The media just *adores* a David and Goliath story. And that's where I plan on waging this war. And let me tell you, the court of public opinion is a bitch."

She straightened, giving him a broad smile.

"Now, you have a nice day."

Not waiting for a reply, she turned on her heel and strolled out of his office.

God*damn*, that had felt good.

Chapter Eighteen

Sweat rolled down Zephirin's face and dripped off his body. His shoulders ached, the muscles in his back burned. And yet, he kept pounding his fist into the punching bag, relishing the vibration that sang up his arms with each impact. Craving the emptying of his mind, the punishment of his body. The punching bag wasn't part of his daily workout routine, but since Saturday, nothing had been normal for him. And lifting weights, squats, and running on the treadmill hadn't granted him the forgetfulness he sought. His mind insisted on thinking. On remembering.

It'd been five days since he'd walked out of Sophia's— no, *Giovanna's*—apartment. Five days since he'd broken his cardinal rule about heavy drinking while training and got shit-faced. The first of three nights, actually. He'd missed the first day of mini-camp, been fined sixty thousand dollars, and hadn't been able to bring himself to care. Though he'd attended the last two days, his performance had been lackluster at best. Thank God no contact work had been involved because as hungover as he'd been, he could've hurt himself or someone else. He could just imagine what was being reported about him and his football readiness on ESPN and the other sports networks. Nothing flattering.

Dom and Ronin had questioned him, then railed at him to get his head out of his ass, to get his shit together. But he couldn't even speak to his friends about the pain that seemed firmly entrenched in his skin, his bones, his very fucking tissue. Couldn't explain the loneliness that crouched inside, waiting for him to close his eyes at night before it sprang and ripped at him. Couldn't voice the anger at himself for letting himself get to this point again. No, not again.

For some inexplicable reason, this pain ran a little deeper. His chest hadn't felt flayed with every drag of breath after he and Shalene had ended their relationship. Hell, he didn't even know if what he and Sophia had could even be called a relationship. He hadn't expected anything to hurt worse than that day in his attorney's office hearing the results of the paternity test. And yet, it did. It could be because his pride had taken another hit at having been played for a fool twice. Or it could be attributed to that he should've known, should've been wiser, but he'd still fallen for the lies with his eyes wide open.

Or maybe it just could be the woman.

The woman had made him excuse the signs he'd sensed so he could have her. So he could touch her a little longer. So he could spend another moment in her presence.

He delivered another punishing blow to the bag, sending it swinging madly on the chain. He'd convinced himself if he hit long enough, hard enough, he could numb his mind along with his body. He could erase those final words spoken in a broken voice from his head: *Good-bye, Zephirin.*

They replayed in an endless loop, and soon his blows matched the rhythm of it. *Good-bye, Zephirin. Good-byeZephirin. GoodbyeZephiringoodbyeZephirin.* His fists flew over and over until the heavy bag danced and the chain jangled.

Eventually, the loud peal of Drake's "Look What You've Done" penetrated the white noise roaring in his ears. He lowered his arms to his side, his chest heaving up and down on his harsh breaths. He didn't need a glance at the cell phone's screen to identify the caller. He'd assigned only one person that ringtone. And as much as he didn't want to talk to anyone, he'd never avoid a call from Josephine Black.

He strode over to the weight bench that he'd tossed the phone on earlier and picked it up, swiping a thumb across the screen.

"Hey, Mama," he greeted, sinking down to the bench. He called his grandmother Mama, not grandma or granny. She'd been his mother most of his life, had given him the stability and family his mother had run away from.

"Hey, Boo," his grandmother replied in the lyrical, deep voice that once boomed down their childhood street, calling him and his sister home before the streetlights came on. In spite of the boulder-sized weight crushing his shoulders and pressing down on his chest, warmth spread through him at the use of her nickname for him. The first time Dom and Ronin had heard his grandmother call him the childhood name, they'd crowed with laughter and teased him mercilessly for months. Bastards. "I haven't talked to you in a few days. Since you seem to have forgotten how to dial my number, I thought I'd give it a try."

"I've just been busy the past few days with mini-camp. I'm sorry about that."

She snorted, apparently not buying his excuse. Not that he believed she would. His grandmother could smell bullshit like a sommelier with wine. "Uh-huh," she drawled. "Who you think you talkin' to, Zephirin Black?" Oh damn. She'd used his given name. He bowed his head, pinching the bridge of his nose. "Now talk to your mama. What's going on? And don't tell me work or nothin'. I know better."

Sighing, Zephirin scrubbed a hand over his head. Talking about his love life to his grandmother ranked up there with having a Brazilian on his balls, but she wasn't going to let it go until he spilled everything. A pit bull had nothing on Josephine Black. "Remember that shoot for the sports magazine I told you about a couple of weeks ago?"

For the next ten minutes, he spoke nonstop, sharing everything with his grandmother about meeting and becoming involved with Sophia Cruz. Well…not everything. If talking about his love life with her was akin to having his balls shaved, talking about *sex* would be like having them chopped off.

After he finished, silence answered him. If not for the sound of *Wheel of Fortune* echoing across the line, he might've thought she had hung up. Finally, a heavy sigh reached him. "I'm sorry, Zephirin. You know I hate that you're hurting. And don't bother trying to deny it, I don't need to be in front of you to know that you are."

He swallowed the denial that had been on the tip of his tongue.

"I never told you this, but I worried so much when you left for college. I can't count how many nights I lay in bed, praying for you," she continued, leaving him shocked by her admission. "You were an itty-bitty thing when your mama left, and even then you tried so hard to be the man of the house. You didn't cry, never said a bad thing about your mama even though God knows she would've deserved every insult. God forgive me for saying that since she's my daughter, but it's the truth." He could imagine his grandmother shaking her head, her long salt-and-pepper hair swinging against her shoulders. "Maybe because she left, you always loved hard. Always tried to protect the people in your life and hold on to them, even when you should've let go." Another sigh. "Too many times you led with your heart instead of wisdom, and I wanted to grab you and shake you. But you were a grown man, so all I could do was pray—pray that you would find someone who would want to take care of you for once. Someone who put your heart and welfare before their own. As much as I love Shalene, she wasn't that person, and I knew it. When everything went to hell with her, I blamed myself for not speaking up."

"Shalene?" Zephirin repeated, reeling from his grandmother's confession. He hadn't known she'd worried about him. And he definitely hadn't known she'd been aware of why he'd broken up with his ex. Of course she knew about the baby, but he'd purposefully kept her in the dark about the rest of it, not wanting to sully her image of the nice girl from down the street. "How did you...?"

She sniffed. "You can't keep anything from me. And besides, that Ronin is like water in a brown paper bag. Can't hold a thing."

Ronin. Zephirin shook his head. Of course. The man had grown up with four sisters and a single mother, and had no defenses when it came to women. All his grandmother probably had to say to his friend was "hi," and the man would've folded like a cheap suit.

"Now don't get mad at him," she chided, as if able to read his mind. Hell, considering the number of times she used to catch him misbehaving as a child, he sometimes believed she had that talent. "You should've been the one to tell me."

"I know how much you love Shalene..."

"And?" she interrupted with a scoff. "Loving someone doesn't mean being blind to their faults. And that child had faults. But you were so intent on saving her, on making up for what had been taken away from her, that you didn't see until it was too late." Her voice softened, and he closed his eyes, squeezing the bridge of his nose harder. "You can't be someone's happiness, baby. And the harder you try, the more that person will come to hate you in the end for failing. That doesn't make Shalene a bad person; it just makes her an unhappy one. And unhappy people can lash out, hurt the ones they love most. But that doesn't sound like your Sophia."

Your Sophia. That resonated in his heart, his soul. A part of him wanted to shut the reaction down, a self-defensive move to protect himself. But the other part—the part that was tired of fighting the denial and hurt, of building walls, of being alone—reached for those words. Grabbed them like leaping for the ball in a game winning touchdown in the end zone. Clutching them to his chest as tight.

"Why do you say that?" he pressed. "She lied to me from day one. How could I trust her?"

"I understand why honesty is so important to you. But Shalene lied to you for personal gain; she stole from you for the same reason. If what you told me is correct, Sophia did all of this for her sister, not herself. And she didn't take from you, she gave. That idea for the app with the camp seemed like a gift to you."

It had been. A precious gift. Not just because it'd been a brilliant idea, but because Sophia had conceived it for him. For *him*. Where Shalene had always asked or demanded what he could do for her, Sophia had freely given without expecting anything in return. Had he become used to someone taking from him that he'd turned jaded, hardened...suspicious?

If you're honest, you would admit you've been waiting for me to fail, to prove you right so you could walk away without any risk, any sacrifice.

Sophia's accusation punched him in the chest, pile-driving the air from his lungs.

She was right. Even as he'd proposed a renegotiation of their terms...even when he couldn't stay away from her...

even when he'd shared the most painful time of his life with her...even during those intimate occasions, hadn't there been a small, dark voice that had whispered, it's only a matter of time? And when the shit hit the fan, hadn't there been the smallest amount of relief, along with the anger and disillusionment, after the torturous waiting for the proverbial shoe to drop was over?

This cynicism, bitterness, and sense of betrayal he knew, was familiar with. And it seemed they'd become his crutches, his shields to justify not risking being hurt again.

Not loving again.

Stepping back, he could see why she'd kept the truth from him. She'd been helping her sister and hadn't planned on their photo shoot meeting evolving into something more. He hadn't either. No, she hadn't known him, hadn't understood that he wouldn't have narc'd her out to *Sports Unlimited*. Their relationship had progressed hot and fast. How could he blame her for not trusting him when he had done the same?

Here I am, Zephirin. Imperfect... Willing to lay myself out there, be naked with you. Tell you I love you.

They'd only known each other for a handful of weeks. If Ronin or Dom had come to him, stating they'd fallen for a woman after such a short amount of time, he would've accused them of having shit for brains before getting them good and drunk.

Yet. He couldn't deny how she twisted him up inside. How—fuck it—happy he'd been with her in his life. How much more content. No. At peace. She made him want. Feel.

Hope.

When it came down to it, was he willing to do the same? To lay himself open, to dive headfirst into that beyond, unsure if he'd have a safety net? Uncertain if he wouldn't break on the rocks?

Was he willing to be as brave?

For Sophia?

Yeah.

But after his angry, bitter tirade a week ago, would she?

"I messed up," he said more to himself than to his grandmother.

"No, baby," she corrected, voice soft. "You fucked up. But I didn't raise no quitter. And if you love her, don't waste any more time than you already have. Go after her."

He'd already decided to, but hearing the hard, don't-take-no-shit note in his grandmother's voice that'd made him hop-to many times in his childhood, he smiled. "Yes, ma'am."

"You bring her home to meet me as soon as possible so I can get a look at her for myself," she ordered.

"Yes, ma'am," he repeated.

"And for the love of God, baby, don't be a knucklehead again, okay? I didn't raise no knuckleheads either."

"Yes, ma'am."

After several more instructions, Zephirin ended the call, his grin slowly fading. Worry crawled inside him, taking up root. The very real possibility that he'd hurt Sophia so deeply she wouldn't be able to hear him, forgive him, struck a twisting fear inside him. In all the years he'd run on that football field, facing down giants who wanted nothing more than to lay him flat on his back, he hadn't experienced fear.

But in all these years, he'd never risked losing something more than a trophy and claim of world champions.

Now, he faced losing the heart of a woman he couldn't imagine enduring another moment without.

He couldn't afford to lose.

Chapter Nineteen

Good God, she was nervous.

Sophia paused in the hallway of the Bellevue three-story building, inches from the frosted glass double doors of Jacobs & Associates Law Offices. She pressed a palm to her belly, inhaling a deep, shuddering breath in the hopes of calming the trample of nerves turning her stomach into their personal stomping ground.

You can do this. You will *do this.*

She'd received a call from the firm two days earlier, requesting a meeting on Saturday morning regarding a project. Stunned didn't accurately capture the shock that had momentarily frozen her, left her speechless on the phone. After all, it'd only been Monday that she'd decided to leave her job with FamFit and venture off on her own. Getting spectacularly dumped by the man one loved did wonders for boosting courage. What could scare her more than confessing her love to a man, and hurt worse than having him reject it *and* her?

Definitely not walking away from a job that had made

her increasingly more disillusioned and suffocated to pursue a dream she'd harbored for years. Yes, she could fail, but at least she would've tried. At least she would be happy and fulfilled with her career.

Okay...happy might be pushing it, but one day. One day, when the memories of Zephirin Black started to fade, she would be. One day, the empty chasm that yawned wide in her chest like a black hole would shrink, and eventually disappear.

In the meantime, she had a plan—contact former clients and let them know she now worked as a freelance app developer, budget the savings she would live on in the foreseeable future, and pray. Hard. And if she had to apply for and accept a job with another company while building her own? Well, she'd do what she had to do. But the next time wouldn't be with management who resented her for her tits and brain.

This meeting was a godsend. Sophia had questioned Giovanna regarding whether or not it was her doing, but her twin had denied it. So, the feelers she'd sent out must've produced results. She'd hoped it would happen, just hadn't expected a response so soon.

"Loitering outside the office isn't going to win points," she grumbled to herself, forcing her trembling legs forward. "Neither is talking to yourself." Marching to the door, she grasped the handle, tugged it open, and entered the elegant lobby before she could chicken out.

She was met with the kind of silence that seemed to encapsulate museums, lecture halls, and IRS offices. Moneyed, reverent, and intimidating. The expensive, wheat-colored carpet smothered any sound of her stiletto heels clicking against the floor as she approached the receptionist's desk. Gold lettering declaring the firm's name curved around the circular, gleaming desk. The slender, perfectly groomed brunette behind the large piece of furniture smiled politely at Sophia.

Thank God she'd raided Giovanna's closet for the tailored black pencil skirt and matching jacket. Note to self: the graphic tees and jeans she'd worn at FamFit wouldn't fly if she intended to compete in the corporate arena.

"Good morning," she greeted the woman whose desk plate identified her as Priscilla. "My name is Sophia Cruz. I have an appointment with Anthony Jacobs."

"Of course, Ms. Cruz." She stood and rounded the desk. "He's expecting you. If you'll follow me." She turned on a sky-high heel and headed down a corridor, leaving Sophia to trail after her.

She could practically smell the wealth in the air, taste it. From the gleaming wood panels and gold molding along the ceilings and floorboards to the shiny brass handles on the thick-looking cherry wood doors, this office boasted clients with deep pockets. Which, she mused as Priscilla paused in front of one of those heavy doors, begged the question of what she was doing there. She didn't doubt her ability to perform whatever job they had, but *they* didn't know that. How could they? A twenty-four-year-old, freshly unemployed app developer didn't appear to be the kind of resume they would hunt up, discover, and exclaim, "Yes, her!" over.

But she stood here now. And she would make damn sure they—whoever "they" were—didn't walk away disappointed.

The receptionist knocked once then opened the door. Murmuring her thanks, Sophia passed by her and entered a large conference room. A long, glass table bisected the area, and black, leather chairs surrounded it. Three men occupied the far side, and she automatically smiled, her arm rising—

Oh my God.

She couldn't move her suddenly numb legs. Couldn't lower her arm. Couldn't push air through her apparently atrophied lungs. *No.* The word whispered through her mind, gathering volume and speed with each ricochet against her skull until a dull roar filled her ears.

Zephirin.

Her paralyzed body didn't prevent her from drinking him in like a dry riverbed after a sweltering summer drought. She'd seen him clothed in just a pair of football pants, T-shirt, jeans, and just the skin God blessed him with. And while nothing could compare to Zephirin Black naked, the three-piece, charcoal gray suit came damn close. The expensive material embraced his body like a shameless lover, emphasizing the width of his shoulders and chest, the strength of his arms, and the muscular grace of his hips and legs. The stylish vest drew attention to his flat abs, and all she could picture was the taut, tattooed skin underneath. Trailing her lips over that flesh. Loving it and him.

It'd been a week since she'd last seen him. A week...an eternity. The impact of seeing him was the same as if it'd been eons. Devastating.

Shock melted and dissolved under the red, pulsing lashes of pain lacerating her heart. Just the sight of him tore off the flimsy scab that helped her cope during her waking hours. His scornful words, fury, and hard expression bombarded her, and she forcefully stiffened her knees, refusing to crumble before him. She'd offered him her heart, her love, and he'd knocked them out of her hands, trampled on them on his way to the door; she refused to hand over her pride, too.

"What are you doing here?" Manners gave way to the hurt and burgeoning anger. Was this some kind of joke? A more horrible, ironic thought slipped through her mind. "Wait. Are you slapping me with some kind of gag order?" She barely suppressed a snort. As if she would give the greedy public and tabloids front row center seats to her humiliation.

A flash of emotion flickered across his otherwise

impassive face. Regret? Pain? Hell no. There she went, trying to convince herself she spied something there that he obviously didn't feel. Not for her.

Firming her resolve and delivering her heart a short but harsh Get With the Program lecture, she shifted her attention to the other two men in the room. Older, they both wore fixed, poker faces. As if they witnessed unpleasant outbursts from potential employees or contractors in their office all the time.

Embarrassment heated her face, and she crossed the space between her and the table, extending her hand toward them. These two might be on his side, but her mother would rail at her if Sophia didn't exhibit the manners she'd been raised with.

"Thank you for coming in, Ms. Cruz." The taller of the two shook her hand first. Dressed in an impeccable black suit and bearing a slight resemblance to Harrison Ford, he gestured to the man next to him. "I'm Anthony Jacobs, and this is my brother and partner, Grant Jacobs." Grant, shorter and a little thicker in frame, nodded. "And I believe you already know Mr. Black."

"It's nice to meet you," she said, not confirming or denying the obvious. *Just keep your eyes on them*, she instructed herself. *Act like he isn't even here.* She could do it; she could pretend she didn't feel his gaze on her. Pretend his presence didn't shrink the size of the room to that of a shoe box.

"Please, have a seat," Grant Jacobs offered, waiting until she lowered into one of the unsurprisingly luxurious leather seats before reclaiming his own. "I'm sure you're wondering why we asked you to come to our office."

Understatement of the year, but she'd go with it. "Yes, I have to admit I am curious." And her voice didn't quiver once, nor did she peek at the silent Goliath to the attorneys' left. Go her.

"Well, we won't keep you in suspense." An almost

pleasant smile warmed Anthony's face as he slid one of two slim stacks of paper across the table toward her. "This is a standard independent contractor agreement. You will want your attorney to read it over with you, but it details the agreement between you and the Jaybird Foundation for the Warrior Nation app—"

"I'm sorry," she interrupted, leaning forward. "The what?" Contract? Her attorney? What were they talking about?

"I took the liberty of naming your app," Zephirin said. Her regard jerked to him, but one meeting with those eagle eyes had her returning her attention to the two lawyers.

"The contract covers a one-time fee for developing the project as well as twenty percent of the income generated from the app, among other points. Also"—he pushed the second sheath forward—"you'll want to have your attorney review this with you as well. This is an investor's agreement for an as-of-now unnamed entity for a future business owned by Sophia Cruz. It's a pretty straightforward venture-capital agreement that outlines protection of the newly formed entity as well as the amount of shares, schedule for distribution of dividends, protection of interests…"

Had she tumbled into an alternate universe? A wormhole? She thrust up a hand, palm out, halting his description of the contract. "An investor's agreement? Venture capital? I don't have investors. I don't even have a venture." She loosed a low chuckle, rife with the disbelief and shock rolling through her. "I mean, I do, but I just decided on it four days ago. Nothing's incorporated yet…" Jesus, she was rambling. "I'm sorry. I'm just a little confused about what's going on."

"Anthony, Grant, if you would give us the room for a moment?" Zephirin said, and as the other two men rose and left the room, part of her wanted to walk out right after them. Or at least beg them not to leave her alone with Zephirin. She wasn't logical when it came to him, and she feared betraying herself.

He dropkicked your heart. Have some damn pride.

The mental reprimand kept her in her chair, forced her to meet his stare.

"What is all this supposed to prove?" she demanded. He'd shoved her away, out of his life, and now he'd set up this meeting with attorneys and contracts and purchase agreements. As a man whose career was playing games, had she become another one for him?

Pain and fury mated into a throbbing heartbeat, and she curled her fingers around the edge of the chair. If he expected her to offer up another pound of flesh, he would be sorely disappointed.

"I spoke with Giovanna a couple of days ago, and she told me about how you were passed over for a position you earned. That would've been the day you showed up late at the high school, wouldn't it?" He didn't wait for her to confirm his assumption. "Why didn't you tell me?"

"Tell you that I, the supposed model, had been shafted by her supervisor at the technology company that my supposed sister, the app developer—which was really me—worked for?" She snorted. "I don't know why in the world I didn't share that with you."

"I would've been there for you," he said, voice low. "I would've wanted to be."

You were. The assertion leaped into her head before she could stifle it. But it was true. He might not have realized it, but by offering to slay her dragons when he didn't even know what they were, he'd gifted her with that comfort. And then he'd granted her the haven of his bed, of pleasure...of the quiet moments afterward where he just held her.

She shook her head, physically trying to dislodge the memories.

"Water under a very old bridge now." But then the earlier part of his statement slammed into her. He'd spoken with Giovanna a couple of days ago? Why would he contact her? *Traitor*, she silently muttered, condemning her twin to a month of their mother's chicken and rice.

"Your sister has a very colorful vocabulary—in both English and Spanish. She hung up on me two times before letting me explain my reason for calling. And she finally agreed to help me only after threatening to rip my balls off and shoving them up my ass if I hurt you."

Okay...so she might forgive Giovanna eventually.

"It's a little late for the hurting me part, isn't it? Is that what all this is about?" She waved a hand over the two contracts. "Well, no worries, Zephirin. A bad breakup isn't going to cause me to fall apart. Can we call it a breakup, though, since we weren't actually together? And since both of us agreed that one of us could end it at any time?" She pursed her lips and tapped a fingertip against them. "Anywho, I'm made of stronger stuff than that, so this parting gift, if that's what it is, really isn't necessary. Are we done here?"

"Let's go ahead and get the business out of the way," he growled, leaning forward and folding his arms on the table.

His gold and green gaze narrowed, his nostrils flaring the slightest bit. Fascinating, witnessing that control and impassivity crack. Like watching a formerly calm lion snarl and swipe at the bars restraining him. A warning that if he was freed, he would pounce.

Arousal hummed through her at the sight. She resented it even as she fought not to squirm in her seat.

"Giovanna told me you'd decided to freelance, start your own company. I'd already decided to contract you for the app development of the project you came up with. In my opinion, no one else was better for the job or would do it better. Even if you still worked for FamFit, I intended to ask you to freelance outside of it. So that isn't charity. It's business. Smart business. As is the investor's agreement." He tapped the table in front of the second sheath of papers. "Once I found out you intended to found your own business, I wanted to be a part of it. Even if you couldn't stand the sight of me, I believe in you, in your passion, your brilliance. That, too, is smart business. I'm not an idiot, and I know a great investment when I see it. *You* are great. And I'm not the only one who believes it. If you'll look at the list of proposed investors, your parents, sister, neighbors, hell, even a couple of my friends are there. I may have contacted them about you venturing off on your own, but I didn't have to browbeat anyone into putting their money where their hearts were with you."

She blinked, rocking back into her chair. Her lips might've parted, but her throat had closed up somewhere between *In my opinion, no one else was better for the job or would do it better* and *I believe in you, in your passion, your brilliance.* So instead, she did as he'd suggested and flipped through the pages of the agreement. Three pages in, she came to the list. God. She blinked some more, fighting the sting of tears.

Joseph and Alicia Cruz. Giovanna Cruz. Her parents and sister. Daniel and Natalia Acosta. Her aunt and uncle. Paola Martin. Her first cousin. Yadiel Bonilla, their long-time neighbor and partner in her father's garage. Toward the bottom, Dominic Anderson and Ronin Palamo. And the last name on the list, Zephirin Black.

$500,000.

Ay Dios mio.

"You...can't," she rasped. "That's too..." She shook her head, shock rendering her nearly speechless. "You can't."

"It's my money," he said, apparently deciphering what she referred to. "And I would've given more." He paused, the intensity in his gaze sharpening, the skin over his cheekbones tautening. "I would give you everything."

"No," she breathed. "You don't get to say that to me." Panic lurched inside her, and she shot to her feet, the leather chair rolling back and hitting the wall. She staggered for the conference room door on unsteady legs. Not caring how desperate or manic she appeared, she grasped the handle, needing out. Away from him and those bright eyes that held the whisper of promises she would've done anything for a week ago. Now...now they just shredded what was left of her heart.

She twisted the handle, but before she could yank it open, a large hand closed over hers. A hard chest pressed to her back. Firm but full lips brushed over the tip of her ear. For an instant, she froze; the shock of his body against her when she'd accepted she would never feel it again momentarily robbed her of the ability to move. But that wild, injured animal inside her chest snapped and clawed, remembering the searing pain his rejection had inflicted. With a small cry, she snatched her hand from under his, jerking away from him and placing much-needed space between them.

"You don't get to touch me either," she said, shoring up the fissures and cracks in her composure that his nearness smashed into like a battering ram.

He didn't follow her but also didn't release her from the power of his gaze. And she couldn't glance away. The traitorous part that missed everything about him didn't want to.

"The last time we saw each other, you could barely stand to look at me, much less touch me. Now, you're offering me my dream on a silver platter and acting like you were never disgusted by me. What changed?" she demanded.

"I was never disgusted by you, Sophia. *Never*," he said, the fierceness of his tone startling her. "And what changed in me? You. You held up a mirror that I had no choice but to stare into, and I didn't like what I saw." He dropped his head for a moment, but when he lifted it, none of the intensity in his eyes had faded. No, it'd increased, deepened. Made his gaze sharper, brighter. Next to his thighs, his fingers curled and relaxed. Curled and relaxed.

"You were right; you never stood a chance with me. Not because you weren't beautiful, giving, selfless, or deserved it. It was all on me—my issues, my hang-ups, my refusal to let go of the past. I had become so accustomed to someone taking from me. Then there was you, asking for nothing—wanting nothing—but me. And even then, I had to convince you to have more. No one has desired me just for me. I didn't trust it, and though I wanted to, didn't trust you. Like you accused me of, a part of me was waiting for you to fuck up, for what we had to fall through. I turned you away out of my own fear, and I'm sorry for it. Where I couldn't offer forgiveness, now I'm asking for yours."

Mouth dry, she stilled, her heart beating a rapid tattoo against her rib cage. When she'd left her apartment this morning, the last thing she'd expected was to have this proud, strong man humble himself. For her. She searched his face, taking in the tension straining the carnal lines of his mouth, the clenching of his jaw. "You always had it," she whispered.

Truth. Even though he'd hurt her like no other, she'd understood why. Comprehended that his pain went beyond the lie she'd spun. Even anger couldn't dispel the stubborn love that, though bruised and battered, refused to dissipate.

"Sophia, take me. Have me." He shifted closer, turning his hands up in the age-old gesture of surrender. "You once said you didn't have my heart, but you still cherished it, would fight for it. I'm telling you, it's yours. You don't have to fight because I'm offering it to you. Begging you to take it. Because if not, I don't have any use for it."

Jesus. She pressed a palm to her chest directly over

her heart as if she could contain the swelling of it, ease the hammering of it against her skin. "You hurt me. I don't know if…" she confessed, the words raking over her throat. "I lied to you, broke your cardinal rule. How can you trust me again? How can I trust you not to throw it up in my face again…?" She shook her head once more. Because she'd managed to get up this time, but if he led her to believe they had a chance—that she could give him her heart—and he rejected it again? The next time might lay her out for good.

"I want to renegotiate," he said, taking another step closer. She couldn't help but remember the last time he'd uttered those words, and how she'd eventually capitulated to them.

"What are you proposing now?" she whispered.

Another step. "One chance for your heart wasn't enough. I didn't get an opportunity to discover everything about you. Didn't get to find out what it feels like to protect it, claim it for my own. So here are the terms." And another step until only inches separated them. "You let me love you until I get my fill. Which, I'm warning you, probably will be never. You don't want strings, a relationship? Not fine. I won't accept anything less than all of you. You want to walk away whenever you're done? Again, not fine. I'll chase you down. But until I can convince you that I'm not going anywhere, just let me have even a little bit of you. And you can have me—all of me—in return."

She squeezed her eyes shut as he recited the words that started their original arrangement…only substituting the words that had her soul singing in hesitant joy. Had her trembling in deferred hope.

"What are the rules?" she breathed.

"You need them?" he asked, tilting his head.

"Yes."

With a deep, low sigh, he cupped her face in his big,

rough palms. And there in his eyes were all the answers that continued to niggle at her.

"I just have one." He touched his forehead to hers. "Love me again."

She covered his hands. And there fell the last of her resistance. Her pain. Turning her face into his palm, she pressed her lips to it. "I never stopped," she confessed.

His lashes lowered, but she didn't need to see his eyes. Not when his body shuddered against hers. Not when his mouth swooped down and seized hers in a kiss that not just claimed her, but mirrored all the love and need swelling inside her. Joy like she'd never known stung her eyes, and the tears she'd managed to hold back all this time, trickled over.

Murmuring, he swept his lips over the signs of her happiness, and when his mouth fused with hers once more, she tasted the slight saltiness and didn't mind. Not when these tears were of love, hope, and the bliss she could barely contain.

"I've missed you," he rasped into the kiss. He dropped his head and hands, buried his face into the nook between her neck and shoulder. "God, I've missed you," he repeated in a harsh whisper that vibrated through her. His fingers flexed against her waist, seeking, greedy.

And answering need flared between her legs. She'd been so empty, had doubted she would ever be filled again. Dipping her head, she recaptured his mouth, thrust her tongue between his lips, conveying without words how much she wanted him. Now. Conference room and attorneys be damned. Just as long as he satisfied the aching hunger deep inside her. Which seemed only fair since he'd been the only man to ever stir it.

Hard fingers fumbled at the buttons of her jacket, almost ripping them off before the lapels opened, and he palmed her breasts through her shirt. Unerringly, he found her piercings and tugged, shooting pain-tinged pleasure down her torso straight to her sex. She arched against him, a cry slipping free. Sliding her fingers beneath his jacket, she clutched his shoulders, her nails digging into his firm, shirt-covered flesh.

Snatching a page out of his book, she released the buttons on his vest and dragged his shirt free of his waistband. More than her next breath, she needed to touch his skin, reacquaint herself. Seven days had been a lifetime.

His growl of pleasure rumbled against her palms, and she imitated his caress, tweaking his small, masculine nipples.

"Damn, I need to be inside you," he half snarled, half groaned. Abandoning her breasts, he gripped the bottom of her fitted pencil skirt and worked it up her thighs. "I thought I'd never be here again. Say yes, baby." If she hadn't already decided to do just that, the desperate, almost frantic edge to the plea shaped as a command would've convinced her. That same damn near violent need to have him inside her, to seal the love that capsized her, washed away all sanity.

"Yes. Now," she breathed, helping him to raise the clothing over her hips. The same hunger for him raged through her, but this time was different. Because before she'd been insecure, not believing she could ever claim this beautiful, powerful man as hers. Didn't believe he would do the same.

Zephirin hiked her up, pinning her between the wall and his body. "Wallet. Jacket. Inside pocket," he rapped the words out, grabbing the band of his pants and zipper. But she didn't need further instructions. Seconds later, his wallet dropped to the floor, and she ripped open the condom she'd recovered from it.

Leaning backward only to slide on the protection, he hooked the panel of her panties to the side and notched his cock at her opening. She shivered, craving him so bad she probably resembled an addict in need of her next hit. But only of him. He was, and always would be, her only drug of choice.

Wrapping her arms around his neck, she pressed her lips to his. The slow penetration of her tongue matched the measured, deliberate penetration of her flesh. They filled one another, giving, taking. Asking, demanding. Loving. Promising.

With a low, almost painful groan, he seated himself fully within her. Stretching her with that delicious, wicked burn that meant he was branding himself inside her. But not just her body this time. Her heart. Her soul.

"I love you, Sophia," he whispered. "So damn much."

Every thrust, every stroke, every drive deep into her body emphasized his vow. When she flew over the edge into the fiery furnace of orgasm, she didn't fear letting go, knowing with every cell of her being that he would catch her. And when his body stiffened against her, his hips smacking hers, plunging his cock deep until he couldn't bury any further, she returned the gift. Holding him, bearing him up.

"I have one last term," he said, brushing a kiss over her jaw, cheekbones, the piercing in her eyebrow before withdrawing from her and carefully lowering her to the floor. Gently, he took care of her and straightened their clothes.

"What's that?" she asked, circling his waist and tipping her head back. He accepted the unspoken invitation and dropped a lingering kiss to her mouth.

"You have to come to New Orleans to meet my grandmother." A wry but full smile curved his lips, and her heart leaped at the beauty of it. "I don't think she's going to let me back in the house if you're not with me. As a matter of fact, she called me this morning to specifically tell me that."

Laughter bubbled up out of her like the sweetest, most potent champagne. This was sheer joy. Squeezing him, she laid her ear over his heart.

This she could get used to.

"Deal."

Epilogue

"Wow," Sophia murmured, leaning her elbows back against the bar at Doyle's. It'd been a couple of days since she'd left the law offices with Zephirin. But so much had happened—a brand new company, investors, capital, her first client, and of course, the man she loved in her life again. For the past two mornings that she'd woken up, curled against Zephirin's big body, she'd prayed it all hadn't been a dream. And each time, when he'd rolled over and pinned her underneath him, his mouth and hands moving over her, she'd grinned, squeezing him tight, knowing this beautiful giant was hers, and this was now her life.

Her unpredictable, walking-out-on-a-limb, calling-her-own-shots-with-a-wonderful-man-beside-her life.

She was like a kick-ass mash-up of Cinderella and Olivia Pope.

"Wow, what?" Zephirin shifted beside her, his chest brushing her shoulder as he angled his body toward her. "And why are you showing all thirty-two teeth?"

Her smile didn't dim. "Twenty-eight, smart-ass. My

wisdom teeth were removed."

"See? I learn more and more about you every day," he said, accepting her margarita from the bartender and passing it to her. He took a sip from his beer. "So what has you grinning so hard?"

"I still can't believe your friends are so nice and welcoming to me." She dipped her head, indicating the small group of men and women across the bar. "I know you assured me they weren't upset with me, but I can't say I'd blame them if they did have a problem."

Zephirin stroked his free hand down her hair, pressing a kiss to the top of her head. "Ronin and Dom invested in your company. They wouldn't have done that if they didn't like you, no matter how talented and brilliant you are. And you make me happy. That's all they care about."

She tilted her head back and brushed a kiss along his jaw. "You make me happy, too."

Sighing, she turned her attention back to his friends... and now hers. Ronin, Dom, Tennyson, and Renee gathered around a low table, laughing and talking. The last member of their circle, Jason, spoke with a couple of people nearby. Zephirin had informed her of how rare it was to have Renee and Jason in the same space together since their friends-with-benefits relationship had resulted in hurt feelings on both sides and a strain on their tight group. Speaking of friends with benefits...

She narrowed her gaze. "Are you sure Dom doesn't know Tennyson is in love with him?" When he erupted into a coughing spasm, she arched an eyebrow. "What? Don't tell me you didn't guess either?"

Zephirin shook his head, frowning as he waved his beer in the direction of the couple under discussion. "You mentioned that when we first met. Sophia, they're best friends. Have been since they were kids. There's nothing else going on between them."

"Men," she muttered. "Maybe you guys are too close to them to notice, but see how she stares at him? It's how I look at you."

A smile softened his expression, and when he lowered his head, she met him halfway. His lips closed over hers, and she opened for him, deepening the kiss that spoke of her love and need for him. And his for her.

"Are you through meeting them?" he growled into her ear.

She grinned, and taking his beer, she set both of their drinks on the bar behind them.

"C'mon," she said, sliding her hand into his and leading him toward the bar exit. "You still haven't given me the full explanation of roughing the tight end."

He snorted. "That's roughing the passer, baby."

"Not in my game, it isn't," she drawled and, stopping just outside the restaurant door, swatted him on the ass.

Laughing, he pinched her chin and planted a firm kiss on her mouth. "I think I like your rules better."

"I figured you would."

Acknowledgments

To my heavenly Father who has never failed me when I've called on Him and even when I haven't. I thank you for being so much bigger than my imagination and supplying my every need.

To Gary. You are my real-life hero, and without your endless support and encouragement, none of this would be possible. We're a writing team, even if my name is the only one on the book covers. LOL!

To Kevin and Autumn. Thank you for coming up with the team name, Washington Warriors! There's your shout out, guys. Although, you'll never see it because if I catch either of you reading my books, I will go all *National Geographic* on you! LOL!

To Andie Rutledge, aka The Seattle Guru. You have been so generous with your time and patient with my many questions, and I'm so grateful! My Seattle tour book is dog-eared! Tell your hubby I said thanks for his input, too! MUAH!!

To Debra Glass. You have never turned me down when I

come knocking for critiques, advice, laughs, whatever I need. You're not just my critique partner, you're my bestie, and I adore you!

To The Football Council, aka Gary, Daddy, Kevin, and Konard. Thank you for always answering your phones when I come to you with my endless football questions. And they have been endless. LOL! I so appreciate your patience...and for giving me dialogue because I had no idea how to call a play...or describe a move...or use a football metaphor. Love you!!

To Marta Baez Petrocelli. Thank you for helping me bring Sophia to life. From the translations, to the traditions, to mannerisms, to coffee, you helped me shape a gorgeous, vibrant, wonderful heroine of Puerto Rican heritage. Thank you!

To Rachel Brooks. Thank you for believing in me as well as offering me guidance, encouragement, or a firm but nice "Put the pizza back in the oven" when I need it. LOL! I'm so proud to claim you as my agent!

To Tracy Montoya. Every time we start a new series, I'm so happy because it means more books we're going to be working on together. You have been so instrumental in my growth as a writer. Thank you for everything you've taught me with each book and for always pushing me to dig deeper and be better. You are THE BEST!

About the Author

Naima Simone's love of romance was first stirred by Johanna Lindsey, Sandra Brown, and Linda Howard many years ago. Well, not that many. She is only eighteen…ish. Though her first attempt at a romance novel starring Ralph Tresvant from New Edition never saw the light of day, her love of romance, reading, and writing has endured. Published since 2009, she spends her days—and nights—creating stories of unique men and women who experience the first bites of desire, the dizzying heights of passion, and the tender, healing heat of love.

She is wife to Superman, or his non-Kryptonian, less bulletproof equivalent, and mother to the most awesome kids ever. They all live in perfect, sometimes domestically challenged bliss in the southern United States.

Come visit Naima at www.naimasimone.com.

THE BAD GIRL AND THE BABY
a *Cutting Loose* novel by Nina Croft

When Captain Matt Peterson finds himself the guardian of his baby niece, he knows he's in over his head. Then he meets the child's aunt—tough, sexy MMA fighter Darcy Butler—and he knows he's really in trouble!

DIRTY GAMES
a *Tropical Temptation* novel by Samanthe Beck

Quinn Sheridan suddenly has half the time she anticipated to turn herself into an action hero for the role of her career. Luckily, her agent calls in a secret weapon, but the demanding, drop dead gorgeous hardass fails to understand *she's* the client. She has no problem taking direction, but Luke's definition of cooperation feels more like complete and utter submission. And she's tempted to give it to him....

CPSIA information can be obtained
at www.ICGtesting.com
Printed in the USA
LVHW04s1734020718
582503LV00001B/76/P

9 781981 757183